Made for Each Other
Irene Brand

Steeple
Hill®

Published by Steeple Hill Books™

STEEPLE HILL BOOKS

Steeple Hill®

ISBN-13: 978-0-373-81362-9
ISBN-10:   0-373-81362-7

MADE FOR EACH OTHER

Printed in U.S.A.

"Is this becoming a habit?" Jacob asked. "We keep running into each other."

"I'm not following you," Aimee said with a low laugh. "I promise. I didn't know you attended this church."

"Yes, and it's great that you're here. Let me find a good seat for you." Once seated, Aimee surreptitiously watched Jacob as he carried out his duties as usher. His voice was compassionate. He was gracious to old and young alike. She noticed again how captivatingly handsome he was, and decided that Jacob's nature matched his appearance.

Was it just coincidence or was it significant that she had encountered him three times in as many days? Her Granny always used the expression, "It was meant to be." Could that be true of her and Jacob?

Books by Irene Brand

Love Inspired

IRENE BRAND

Writing has been a lifelong interest of this author, who says that she started her first novel when she was eleven years old and hasn't finished it yet. However, since 1984 she's published more than thirty contemporary and historical novels and three nonfiction titles. She started writing professionally in 1977 after she completed her master's degree in history at Marshall University. Irene taught in secondary public schools for twenty-three years, but retired in 1989 to devote herself to writing.

Consistent involvement in the activities of her local church has been a source of inspiration for Irene's work. Traveling with her husband, Rod, to all fifty states, and to thirty-two foreign countries has also inspired her writing. Irene is grateful to the many readers who have written to say that her inspiring stories and compelling portrayals of characters with strong faith have made a positive impression on their lives. You can write to her at P.O. Box 2770, Southside, WV 25187 or visit her Web site at http://www.irenebrand.com.

For if you forgive men when they sin against you,
your heavenly Father will also forgive you.
—*Matthew* 6:14

To the youth of Harmony Baptist Church

Chapter One

"You're going to do what?"

Aimee Blake pivoted quickly away from the vanity where she was applying her makeup and stared at her daughter. With a bulging backpack slung over her shoulder, Samantha leaned carelessly against the doorjamb, her face serene, as if she hadn't just tossed a bombshell in her mother's lap.

"I'm going to ride to school with Jennifer. She's picking me up."

"Why?"

"Duh—because she can drive now," Samantha said, avoiding her mother's stare. "Jennifer's parents bought her the most awesome car. I'll just ride to school with her from now on."

"Without asking me if it's okay?"

Samantha rolled her heavily made-up, smoky-

gray eyes, too heavily made up for Aimee's taste. "Puh-leeze, Mom. I'm not a kid anymore."

"Well, at fourteen, you aren't an adult, either," Aimee stated decisively. "Besides, Jennifer hasn't had her driver's license more than a month."

Samantha shrugged dismissively. "So? She hasn't gotten a ticket. Proves she's a safe driver."

Aimee stifled a grin. Even in her frustration, she was amused at Samantha's adolescent reasoning. Before she could discuss it any further with Samantha, Jennifer Nibert's screeching tires announced her arrival as she sped into the driveway. A slamming car door indicated that she was on her way to the house.

"You can go with Jennifer this morning, but we'll discuss the future tonight," Aimee said quietly. She stepped into the hallway a second before the front door opened and Jennifer wandered inside. As usual, Aimee was startled by the girl's appearance. She was dressed totally in black, except for the silver chains around her waist and neck. Aimee counted four earrings in her left ear, two in the other one. Heavy makeup disguised Jennifer's beautiful facial features and gold-green eyes.

"Ready, Sam? We've got to go. Oh, hi, Mrs. Blake. Come and see my new car."

With an inward sigh, Aimee stepped out on the

porch. Jennifer pointed with pride to the two-door blue sports car parked in the driveway. "Pretty sweet ride, huh, Mrs. B.?" she asked Aimee.

"It's awesome!" Samantha agreed. "I love it already."

Although Aimee was worried at the thought of a girl as seemingly immature as Jennifer being turned loose in that car and with Samantha in it, she admitted, "It's very pretty. But it isn't a toy, Jennifer, so drive carefully."

"I always do," Jennifer said, and a beaming grin crossed her friendly, if a little scary-looking, face.

The two girls slid into the leather-covered bucket seats and fastened their seat belts. Jennifer threw the car into Reverse and backed toward the street, then stopped abruptly.

Samantha rolled down her window. "Hey, Mom. I forgot to tell you. I'm going to a sleep-over at Jennifer's tonight. Okay? Bye." She closed the window and Jennifer quickly backed into the street and sped away.

This announcement, coming on top of her daughter's surprise decision to stop riding to school with her, was more than Aimee could stomach. Her first reaction was anger, but the shock of Samantha's sudden independence—or was it rebellion?—yielded quickly to concern. Aimee hadn't suspected her daughter of deceiv-

ing her before, but she was convinced now that Samantha had deliberately waited to tell her about the sleepover after she thought it would be too late for her mother to forbid it.

Aimee wiped away the angry tears that threatened to spill from the corners of her eyes as she returned to the house. The pain in her heart was beyond tears. Was she losing her daughter, or was Samantha just growing up?

Glancing at the clock, she knew she didn't have time to fret about the situation now. She had to be at work in forty-five minutes. She rushed into the bedroom to finish dressing for the day. Feeling in need of an extra boost to her self-confidence, Aimee sprayed on some expensive perfume she'd recently bought as a gift to herself. The aromatic lavender fragrance swirled around her as she left the house. Dreading the workday, Aimee drove out of the cul-de-sac where she'd lived for several years.

With a few minutes to spare, Aimee arrived at Eastside Elementary School where she had worked as a secretary ever since the year Samantha had started kindergarten there. As she parked, Aimee glanced across the street to the high school where her daughter was now a student. Where had the time gone? She saw Jennifer's car in the parking lot and breathed a sigh of relief that they'd arrived safely.

Aimee glanced in the side mirror as she stepped out of the car, noting that her brows were drawn together and her lips were drawn tight, too. She couldn't greet her co-workers and the children looking as uptight as she felt, so she forced herself to put on a smile. Her efforts fell a little short, but at least she looked slightly more pleasant as she hurried toward the door.

She slowed her steps when she encountered a tall, muscular, nicely dressed man leading a boy with a backpack toward the building. At the door, the man turned and saw Aimee. His mouth parted in a smile that highlighted the most attractive face Aimee had seen in a long time. His elegant, handsome features hinted at a vital power that attracted her. A swath of curly hair hung casually over his smooth forehead.

"Good morning," he said, standing aside to let her enter first.

"Thanks, and good morning to you, too," she answered, hopefully sounding more pleasant than she felt. Aimee thought she knew all the parents, but she was sure she hadn't seen this man before. He wasn't the kind of man one would easily forget. She glanced at the boy. She didn't recognize him either. Judging from the little guy's anxious expression, Aimee figured he probably was a new student.

"Do you work here?" At Aimee's nod, the man continued. "Alex needs an entrance permit for being absent several days," the man said. So the boy was already enrolled. Odd that she'd never seen him. "Where can we get it? He has a doctor's excuse."

"I can arrange that for you," Aimee assured him. "The office is down this hallway." She motioned to the hall on her right.

"Good," the man said. "C'mon, Alex."

The man held the office door for Aimee. She pointed to a row of chairs against the wall of the reception area, saying, "Just take a seat here for a few minutes until I boot up my computer. We'll have Alex on his way to class soon."

She went to her desk, laid down her purse and coat, and booted up the computer. She motioned to the pair to come into her office and take the seats in front of her desk.

"What's your last name, Alex?"

The boy mumbled something, but she didn't understand what he said. She lifted questioning eyes to the man who watched the boy with a tender, brown-eyed gaze.

He laid his arm on the boy's shoulder. "This is Alex Putney. Give the lady your doctor's excuse, Alex."

Checking her computer records, Aimee noticed that Alex had been a student since the first of the year. He pulled a crumpled piece of paper from his pocket and handed it to Aimee. The excuse for nine days had been written by a reputable doctor, so Aimee filled in the permit to send the child back to class.

"There you go, Alex," she said as she handed him the paper. "Sorry you've been sick."

The man Aimee had assumed was Alex's father reached across the desk to shake her hand. His fingers were warm and firm as they gripped hers, and the friendly smile he gave her suddenly wrapped Aimee in warmth. At the door of her office, he turned toward her, smiled again and said, "Have a nice day."

Aimee wasn't anticipating a good day, but it lifted her spirits some just to have someone wish she would.

Throughout the morning as she answered the phone, directed calls and entered report-card information into the computer, she thought of the thick, curly brown hair and dark eyes of the man who'd greeted her so warmly. As she thought about him, her day brightened a bit.

But as her eyes scanned the computer screen and her hands moved automatically across the keyboard, uppermost in Aimee's mind was the "new" Samantha. Aimee had known the day would come when her daughter would broaden her horizons, but she wasn't convinced that either of them was ready for it yet. She took her role as a single parent seriously. *Too seriously?* she wondered. She didn't think so. At barely fourteen, Samantha still needed a great deal of parental supervision, didn't she? More than anything, Aimee wanted to be a good mother, and she was worried about the path Samantha might be heading down.

Lisa, the financial secretary, stopped by Aimee's desk. "I don't know about you, but I'm glad we have the afternoon off. I'm bushed." Lisa slanted a curious glance at Aimee. "You don't look so good either."

"I'm all right." She glanced at the clock. "Only another hour. It does give us a nice break when they have county-wide in-service workshops for elementary teachers."

"Got any plans for the afternoon?"

"The weekly grocery shopping, but I may hold that off until tomorrow."

When Aimee put her fingers back on the keyboard, Lisa took the hint. "See ya," she called as she returned to her office.

An hour later when Aimee left the building, a long afternoon loomed before her. Normally, she would be planning dinner on her way home, but unless she put her foot down and told entered the house, it seemed unusually quiet, and she thought sadly that she might as well get used to it.

"Oh, for cryin' out loud," she muttered. "Stop feeling sorry for yourself. Look on the bright side. For fourteen years, Samantha hasn't given you any trouble, so count your blessings and deal with each situation as it comes."

Through the window, she saw her friend Erica Snyder driving into her garage. Momentarily, she wished that she could be as calm about life as her neighbor, who had a tendency to shrug off trouble when it came her way.

When the phone rang a few moments later, Aimee figured it was Erica, who must have seen Aimee's car in the driveway.

"Hi," Erica said cheerfully. "Tonight is our singles get-together at church. There's going to be a good program. Want to go?"

Erica was constantly trying to fix Aimee up, and she often invited Aimee to go with her to this monthly meeting at Memorial Church. She'd always turned down the invitation before, but now that Samantha was getting independent, perhaps the time had come for her to try something new.

"All right. I will." As soon as the words were

Silence greeted her for a moment. "Well, not that I'm unhappy that you're finally going with me," Erica said, "but I *am* curious. Why the change of heart?"

"Samantha is going to a sleepover tonight, and I don't want to stay home alone."

"Great! The meeting starts at seven. I'll pick you up at six-thirty."

After Erica hung up, Aimee sat at the table and stared into space. "Now, why did you do that?" she finally said aloud. For a moment she considered calling Erica and telling her she'd changed her mind, but Aimee didn't want to disappoint her friend. For the first time, Aimee realized that she'd been so intent on making a good life for her daughter that she didn't really have a life of her own. Maybe it was time to change that.

Appraising herself critically in the mirror, Aimee decided that her long black hair needed a trim. And as she surveyed her image, she suddenly thought of the man she'd met at school this morning. He'd been dressed impeccably in a dark gray suit, white shirt and a navy tie. Aimee fleetingly wondered what he had thought of her. Had he even noticed her? She hadn't even gotten his name.

Making up her mind quickly, Aimee called her hairdresser, who said she could work Aimee in. Two hours later, Aimee wondered if she'd taken leave of her senses when she came out of the mall with a short layered bob and a new outfit.

She was in the bedroom looking at her purchases when Samantha and Jennifer breezed into the house at four o'clock.

"Hey, Mom," Samantha called. "I'm home."

Aimee walked down the hall to meet them.

"Hello, Mrs. Blake," Jennifer said. "You look awesome."

Aimee was pleased at Jennifer's comment, since obviously Samantha hadn't noticed. "I had a trim this afternoon. The hairdresser also shampooed and styled my hair, which always relaxes me."

"That's what my mom says. I fix my own hair unless I need color."

Aimee compared Jennifer's black, Gothic hairstyle with her daughter's long, natural blond hair worn in a high ponytail. Aimee's refusal to allow Samantha to wear her hair like Jennifer's was another recent source of friction between them.

"Don't you think your mother's hair looks cool, Sam?"

With a careless shrug of her shoulders, Samantha said, "Kind of. It doesn't look like you, Mom. Hey, I need snacks and drinks for the sleepover. You can fix me some stuff while I get my things ready. C'mon, Jen. Help me pack."

Samantha seemed tense, as if she expected Aimee to stop her from going to the sleepover. Aimee was annoyed at her daughter's demanding attitude. She could have at least said "please." As she opened the refrigerator door, Aimee wondered what would happen if she did tell Samantha that she couldn't go. Afraid that her daughter would go anyway, Aimee wasn't ready to put her to the test.

As she scanned the refrigerator, Aimee knew she should have gone to the grocery store rather than the hairdresser. Well, it was too late now. She didn't have time to buy groceries and be ready when Erica wanted to leave. She gathered some chips, cookies and pop and put them in a basket.

Samantha's room was on the ground floor of their split-level home, and Aimee walked to the head of the stairs and called, "Your snacks are ready. You're welcome."

Her new clothes lay on the bed, but her daughter's rotten attitude dimmed Aimee's pleasure in the beige linen pants and jacket. She put on the loose-fitting pants, pulled a white cotton tee over her head and slipped into the buttonless jacket, which featured white trim on the cuffs and lapel. She searched in her jewelry box and chose a gold chain and matching earrings, a gift from Steve when they'd become engaged. She still missed him.

Glancing in the floor-length mirror, Aimee scrutinized her appearance. She looked okay, but she still wished she hadn't agreed to go with Erica because she dreaded telling Samantha where she was going. When she heard the girls coming upstairs, Aimee walked into the hallway.

"I'll be out for a few hours this evening."

Samantha whirled around and looked at her mother. "Excuse me? Since when do you have somewhere to go on Friday night?" Her long hair was hanging loose now, and with a quick flip of her fingers, Samantha brushed it away from her face.

"Since I decided to go to a meeting with Erica."

"What kind of meeting?"

Aimee definitely didn't like her daughter's attitude now. She should be quizzing Samantha about *her* evening activities, not the other way around. But she wouldn't embarrass Samantha by reprimanding her in Jennifer's presence. Still, she couldn't tolerate this sort of behavior, and she would deal with it later. With a sinking heart, she wondered what Steve would think if he knew she had allowed their daughter to develop such a belligerent attitude.

As kindly as she could, Aimee said, "It really isn't any of your business where I'm going."

Although her nerves were on edge, Aimee felt like laughing at the look of disbelief spreading across Samantha's face.

"What is with you, Mom?" Samantha demanded.

"Nothing is with me. I have a right as an adult to have my own plans, but I don't mind telling you where I'll be," Aimee said tensely. "However, it would have been nice if you'd asked me in a more civil tone. I'm going to a singles meeting at Erica's church."

"That's cool!" Jennifer said. "Go for it, Mrs. B."

But Aimee could tell by looking at her daughter that she didn't think it was cool. Was it anger or fear she detected in Samantha's eyes?

"You're kidding, right?"

Aimee shook her head. "No. Erica invited me, and since you're going to be away overnight, I couldn't see any reason to spend the evening alone. What time will you be home tomorrow?"

"I don't know," Samantha said sullenly and picked up the basket of food.

Lifting her perfectly groomed eyebrows, Jennifer glanced sideways at her friend before she said, "I've got a dentist appointment at nine o'clock, Mrs. Blake. I'll drop her off before then."

Surprisingly, Jennifer was a polite, seemingly well-behaved girl, and Aimee wondered if she had been judging the older girl too harshly based on her looks. She blamed Jennifer for a lot of Samantha's recent rebellious ways, but perhaps it was time to place the blame squarely on Samantha.

"Thanks," Aimee said to Jennifer. "Have fun tonight," she added.

Samantha didn't answer, but Jennifer said, "That's a cool outfit, Mrs. Blake. See ya tomorrow."

Apparently Samantha hadn't noticed what her mother had on. She turned and assessed Aimee's new clothes suspiciously, casting another critical glance at her mother before she gave an impatient shrug and tossed her long blond hair defiantly. She left the house without a word and slammed the door behind her.

Aimee dropped into the lounge chair before the window in the family room and covered her face with her hands. She heard the chickadees and nuthatches at the feeder outside the window, but she didn't look up. Watching the pretty little birds usually lifted her spirits, but not now when her mind reeled with confusion. Soon her confusion turned to anger—not only at Samantha but also at herself. For years she had catered to her daughter's every whim, so what could she expect?

She clenched her jaw to stop the tears in her heart from reaching her eyes. She would address Samantha's rebellion later, but she wouldn't let this evening be ruined. She *needed* a night out.

Later, when she heard Erica's car horn, Aimee pasted a smile on her face and left the house.

"Well, don't you look sharp!" Erica exclaimed when Aimee opened the car door and sat beside her. "That's a beautiful suit."

Aimee fastened her seat belt, and Erica pulled away from the sidewalk. "I haven't bought any clothes for months, so I went shopping today," Aimee said. "How do you like my hair?"

"Gorgeous! It takes years off of your age." Erica eyed her sharply. "But your eyes are pink. Been crying?"

"You're too observant," Aimee answered with a sigh. "Samantha wasn't happy when she heard where I was going."

"So…" Erica persisted.

"So I've made up my mind to start cutting the apron strings, and I don't mean to separate Samantha from me. She's already done that," Aimee said. "I'm beginning to cut myself loose from her."

"It won't be easy," Erica said sympathetically. "But for your own good, as well as Samantha's, it's time. In only a few years, she'll be off to college."

"I hope so, but it's hard. I feel like I haven't been a good mom, or Samantha wouldn't be so rebellious."

"Oh, it isn't you," Erica assured her. "It's part of growing up. Just keep praying for Samantha."

"Yes, I intend to," Aimee said, although her prayer life was something else she'd neglected in the past few years.

Twenty minutes later, Erica bypassed the brick church building facing Madison Street and drove to an adjacent one-story metal structure housing a fellowship hall and classrooms.

"Please don't make a big deal out of my coming to this meeting," Aimee said. "I may never visit again, so I don't want to call a lot of attention to myself."

Erica's eyebrows arched provocatively.

"I'm serious," Aimee said.

"I'll be good," Erica promised as she got out of the car and walked toward the building. "I'm so happy to see this change in you that I won't do anything you don't like."

Following her, Aimee took a deep breath, suddenly nervous and wishing she had stayed home. As they walked down a short hallway, Aimee lagged behind Erica. Hearing the mingled voices of many people and occasional bursts of laughter, Aimee wondered what she was getting herself into.

"Ready?" Erica asked as they neared a doorway.

Taking a deep breath and squaring her shoulders, Aimee nodded.

Chapter Two

Several times throughout the day Jacob Mallory thought of the secretary he'd met at the elementary school this morning. As he counseled clients at his counseling service, the memory of her sweet, lavender scent nearly distracted him more than once. Aimee Blake, he'd noticed on the nameplate that rested on her desk. Although he'd lived in the small town of Benton for most of his life, he had never met her, which made him wonder if Aimee was new to town.

He worked late and went directly from work to the singles meeting, and as he drove the ten blocks, he thought again of Aimee, the woman with the gleaming dark hair and dark-blue eyes. The long lashes that framed her eyes created a stunning effect offset by her creamy complexion. But he thought he also sensed raw hurt flickering in those blue eyes, and he wondered what had caused her pain.

When he saw Aimee walk into the room with Erica Snyder, Jacob took a deep breath of utter astonishment. Momentarily, he wondered if he was dreaming or wide awake. But when the aromatic scent of lavender wafted toward him, Jacob knew that the woman with Erica was the same one he'd met this morning—the one who had distracted him all day.

When she entered the room with Erica, Aimee saw that it wasn't as daunting as she'd thought. It had fewer than thirty people, and several strips of fluorescent lights shed light on the area. At one end was a kitchen, separated from the main room by a serving window. A podium and an electric keyboard were located at the opposite end of the room.

Two men stood near the entryway. Something seemed familiar about the muscular shoulders of one of them, and when he turned, Aimee recognized the friendly man she'd met at school earlier in the day. He must have recognized her, too, because he stared at her with a look of surprise. By the time they reached him, an infectious smile that spread to his dark eyes had stretched across his face.

"Well, hello again," he said.

Surprised at how pleased she was to see him, Aimee returned his smile. "I didn't expect to see you again, either, at least not so soon." She felt her face flushing. She hoped her remark didn't sound as if she'd been thinking about him.

Aimee sensed Erica's sharp glance. "Say, do you two know each other?"

"Not really," Aimee said. "We met at school this morning, and we haven't even been properly introduced."

"I can take care of that," Erica said. "Aimee Blake, this is Jacob Mallory."

"It's great to see you," Jacob said, moving closer and extending his hand. "Thanks for being so kind to my friend Alex today. He's a shy kid."

She placed her hand in Jacob's and welcomed the warm pressure of his hand grasping hers. This morning she had assumed he was Alex's father, but apparently he wasn't. Then why had he brought the little boy to school?

"I'll introduce you to the others before the meeting starts," Erica said, and Aimee and Jacob exchanged polite smiles as she followed Erica. Walking from one group to the other, Erica kept up a low commentary about the people in the room. Aimee was grateful for the information, hoping she would be able to associate names with faces. They finally sat in a row of chairs not far from the podium. Soon, Jacob stopped beside Aimee and Erica.

"Hi, is it okay if I sit with you?"

"Sure," Erica said. "I have to help set up the stage for our musicians when they get here. You can visit with Aimee while I'm doing that."

As Jacob took the chair to her right, Aimee sensed that Erica wasn't too excited about his sitting with them. She slanted a curious glance toward Erica but couldn't read her expression. For months, Erica had been trying to get Aimee "out of her shell," as she often described it, and Aimee would have thought Erica would be pleased to have Jacob Mallory befriending her. But Erica evidently wasn't keen on leaving her in Jacob's company, and Aimee couldn't imagine why.

In Aimee's opinion, Jacob seemed like a really nice guy—and he wasn't bad to look at either. Again, she noted the tall, well-built man's thick, brown hair and dark brown eyes. His chiseled face was lean with a well-proportioned nose and a large, shapely mouth. Even more important than his physical appearance, he appeared to have a genuine interest in the people around him that instantly put Aimee at ease.

"Have you and Erica just met?" he asked.

"No. We've been neighbors for several years."

"I can't believe she's waited this long to bring you to our meetings," Jacob commented.

"Oh, she's invited me lots of times," Aimee answered, "but I've always refused."

Jacob's brows lifted inquiringly, but Aimee didn't feel like explaining her lack of interest in a singles group. When she remained silent, he said, "Tell me about yourself, Aimee."

Grimacing, she said, "I'm a widow with a fourteen-year-old daughter, going on twenty."

Jacob chuckled as if he understood what she meant, and Aimee added, "Samantha is spending the night at a friend's, so when Erica invited me to this meeting, I came as her guest. I don't intend to join the group."

"I'm sure you'll enjoy it," Jacob suggested.

"Probably, but my main job is being a mother. I started working at Eastside Elementary years ago when Samantha started there, so my job and being a single mom keep me plenty busy. How about you? Are you a native of Benton?"

"Except for four years in college and a few years at a job in the eastern part of Virginia, I've always lived in Benton. I'm a professional counselor. I moved back home when I had the opportunity to buy a counseling service here."

"I assumed that Alex your son," Aimee commented.

"I don't have many relatives," Jacob said, his smile vanishing as he looked slightly disturbed, slightly wistful. "Alex is just a boy I'm trying to help. He's been sick and had to miss several days of school. His mother is ill, too, and she asked me to take him back to school and explain his absence. I met him through Substitute Siblings."

"Substitute Siblings?"

"It's a fairly new organization," Jacob explained. "In my line of work, I see a lot of children from dysfunctional families who are growing up without much love or guidance. The goal of Substitute Siblings is to pair these children with older adults who will be buddies to them."

"Sort of like the Big Brothers Big Sisters volunteers?" Aimee asked.

"Similar to that," Jacob said. "And because there wasn't a branch of that organization in Benton, my grandmother and I decided to start something. In a few cases our volunteers take the children into their homes on a temporary basis, but mostly they just befriend them by taking them shopping, to ball games, to movies or to other activities to make them feel wanted."

The chairman of the group rapped for attention. "Ladies and gentlemen, it's time to start our meeting. Let's come to order, please."

"It sounds like a worthwhile cause," Aimee whispered.

"I think so," Jacob answered. "If you're interested, I'd like to talk with you further about it."

"I'm interested."

Aimee tore a sheet from the notebook she carried in her purse and wrote her phone number and address on it. She handed the paper to Jacob. He folded it and put it in his pocket as they turned their attention to the entertainment for the evening—a band that played popular praise and worship songs.

Aimee enjoyed the music, but throughout the program, she kept thinking about the man sitting next to her. He said he didn't have many relatives. Did that mean his parents weren't living, or did they live elsewhere? And why had her question about family disturbed him?

But she was more puzzled that she hadn't heard of Jacob before this. She judged that he was about her age, and if he had lived in Benton most of his life, why hadn't she met him? Until her marriage she had lived a few miles outside of Benton, but she'd attended school in town. Benton wasn't big enough for their paths not to have crossed before.

When the meeting adjourned, Jacob stood, turned to Aimee and smiled. "Is it all right if I call you later?"

"Sure," she said as Erica nudged Aimee and nodded toward the door.

As they said their goodbyes, several people invited Aimee to become a part of the group. Although she'd enjoyed the evening, she wasn't ready to commit to anything. Besides, she wasn't sure how she would feel about regularly seeing Jacob Mallory. His presence kindled feelings she hadn't experienced for a long time—emotions that she didn't welcome. The less she saw of him the better off she would be.

"Did you have a good time?" Erica asked as she drove away from the church.

"To my surprise, I really did. Thanks for inviting me."

"You're welcome," Erica said tersely.

Aimee shot a surprised glance in her friend's direction. "What's the matter with you? I thought you *wanted* me to break out of my shell, try my wings and all that other advice you've handed out."

"My advice was good, but my plan backfired," Erica said wryly. "You picked up the wrong man."

"Jacob Mallory is the wrong man?" Aimee stammered, shocked by Erica's words. "Besides, I didn't pick him up—you introduced him to me. Regardless of that, I thought he was a really nice guy."

"He is, but I hoped you would find someone and form a *permanent* relationship. There are two or three men in our group who would like to get married if they could find the right woman," Erica insisted.

"That still doesn't explain why you object to Jacob," Aimee exclaimed, puzzled. "I just sat next to the man and talked with him—that's hardly a prelude to matrimony. What's wrong with him? Who is he, anyway?"

Erica pulled into Aimee's driveway and turned off the car's engine. "Jacob Mallory dates women occasionally, but if they start getting serious, he doesn't call them anymore. He apparently isn't interested in a long-term commitment."

"So what. Neither am I. Besides, he didn't even ask me for a date."

"I heard him say he'd call you," Erica pointed out.

"Yes, about the Substitute Siblings organization," Aimee retorted, a little irritated with her friend. "He was talking about it when the meeting started. If I want to get involved in community service, it sounds like a worthwhile way to spend my time."

"That's true—they do tons of good projects. I know you think I'm butting in," Erica apologized, "but I want you to be happy. I don't want you to get hurt through anybody I bring into your life."

"I won't get hurt! I'm content with my life as it is right now. At least, I was until Samantha surprised me with her attitude today." Aimee opened the car door. "Thanks for asking me to go. I had a good time."

Aimee got out of the car, and Erica waited until she stepped up on the back porch and went into the kitchen before she drove away. Aimee locked the door behind her just as the phone rang.

"Hey, Mom," Samantha's voice answered her hello.

"Hey, yourself. Is anything wrong?"

"No, I was checking to see if you were home."

Although slightly irritated, Aimee laughed. "I'm home, Samantha. You didn't need to worry about your old mom."

"Well, I was just wondering," Samantha said sullenly.

"I'm home and going to bed, which I hope you're doing soon, too."

"Goodbye, Mom," Samantha said.

"Goodbye, honey." But Samantha had already hung up.

Aimee walked down the hall to her bedroom to change out of her new clothes and into pajamas. She sat down in the rocking chair beside the bed and picked up the picture of Steve that stood on the nightstand. How many times since his death had she looked at his picture wishing he was still with her? Usually just looking at his face, so much like Samantha's, brought her peace. But not tonight. Tonight, she felt that something, something more than the loss of Steve was missing in her life, and she wondered what the future held.

Restless, Aimee went into the family room and sat in a lounge chair, feet elevated, staring into the darkness. She thought once again about how unfair the aneurysm was that had caused her husband's sudden death. One morning he had gotten up full of life and love, twelve hours later he was gone, leaving her with regrets that she couldn't overcome—regrets she had tried to put behind her for fifteen years.

She had only been nineteen when she and Steve had married, and a year later she'd given birth to Samantha. She hadn't had an easy pregnancy. There were months of morning sickness that even nausea pills didn't help, and during that time she dreaded the intimacies of marriage. Perhaps Steve had sensed this, for he hadn't made any demands on her.

And Samantha's birth was an ordeal, too. Aimee was in the delivery room for over twelve hours, and the birth resulted in a small tear that an incompetent doctor didn't take care of properly. She was so miserable that she didn't share Steve's bed when she came home, and when he died suddenly, she was devastated that she'd concentrated on her own needs rather than his.

Her remorse over how she'd failed Steve only

added to the sorrow she felt after his death. Aimee had never admitted her guilty feelings to anyone, but they had certainly kept her from considering a relationship with any other man. Now, more than a decade of regret seemed like enough. Remembering how easy it was for her to talk with Jacob tonight, she wondered if it was time to put the past behind her and start a new life.

Aimee yawned widely and went back to her bedroom. She got into bed, turned out the light and snuggled under the blankets. Her body was weary, but her mind was wide awake. Where could she go for the guidance she so desperately needed—for Samantha and for herself?

If any of you lacks wisdom, he should ask God, who gives generously to all without fault, and it will be given to him.

Aimee bolted upright in bed, wondering why those words had come to her now. Why had she remembered that particular phrase? Convinced that the words were in the Bible, Aimee turned on the light again. It had been a few years since she had seriously considered her relationship with God, although there had been a time when the church was an important part of her life.

She went to the walk-in closet in the hallway and stepped up on a stool. A Bible was at the bottom of a large stack of Samantha's schoolbooks. Being careful not to topple the whole heap, Aimee pulled the Bible free. It was Steve's Bible, and she was sure she could find what she wanted in it.

Carrying the Bible, she returned to bed. After a half hour of searching, she found the verse she'd remembered in the Book of James.

As she turned the pages of the Bible, she felt Steve's presence more keenly than she had for years. To her surprise, she also sensed the presence of God. Tears slid down Aimee's cheeks as she remembered when the Word of God had been an important part of her life—when she never started a day without reading the Word. She had gradually drifted away from her faith.

God, it's been so long since I've talked to You, I hardly know what to say. For starters, I suppose I should ask forgiveness for the way I've neglected You for years. I understand now that serving You should have been primary in my life. I should have encouraged Samantha to follow You, instead of putting school and activities before everything else. Starting tomorrow, with Your help, I'm going to change that.

When she laid the Bible on the nightstand, Aimee was relaxed enough to go to sleep. As she again settled into bed and turned off the light, she knew it wouldn't be easy to live up to her new resolve in the light of day. But she was going to try.

By the time Aimee woke up, she had settled on her plan of action. Knowing that her relationship with Samantha hadn't deteriorated overnight and that it would take time to heal, she would go slow, but she also needed to be firm. The stakes were too high to make more mistakes.

As she dressed for the day, she remembered Jacob Mallory. Would he be a complication in the new beginning she contemplated?

Chapter Three

Aimee turned off the vacuum when she heard the door slam. Samantha plodded into the family room through the front door, dragging the bag that held her stuff. She was still in pajamas. Some of her hair was in the ponytail holder, the other half hung loose around her shoulders. Her half-closed eyes were a pretty good indication that the girls stayed up all night.

"Hi, honey," Aimee said. "How was the sleepover?"

As she slouched toward the steps that went to her downstairs room, Samantha mumbled something Aimee didn't understand. Aimee let it go and moved the vacuum into her bedroom, when Samantha yelled from downstairs, "Mom!"

Aimee went to the head of the open stairway, "Yes?"

"I'm trying to sleep," Samantha said. "Pu-leeze! Vacuum some other time."

"I always vacuum on Saturday morning," Aimee replied. "I'll be through in a half hour."

Aimee finished vacuuming and started dusting. Usually, she crept around the house so she wouldn't wake Samantha, but she made no effort to keep quiet today.

The telephone rang and Samantha didn't pick up her extension, so Aimee answered.

"Hi," Erica said, "just checking to see how you're doing this morning."

"Okay, I guess. Samantha is still in bed. I don't suppose she slept at all last night. It's time to have a talk with her, and I want her wide awake when that happens so I'm letting her sleep in. But I'm glad you called. What time is worship at your church tomorrow?"

"There's an eight-thirty service and one at ten-thirty. I go to the later one. Do you want to come with me?" Erica said quickly, obviously pleased. She had asked Aimee to go to church so often that she'd given up.

"I am going tomorrow, but I'll drive. I intend to give Samantha the option of coming with me, but I'm not expecting her to. Would you mind waiting for me at the church door, so I won't have to sit alone?"

"I'll watch for you in the foyer," Erica said. "Good luck with your mother-daughter talk."

"Thanks, I'll need it."

Jacob dressed in his running shoes and a pair of sweats, drew on a lightweight windbreaker and let himself out of the apartment he rented in his grandmother's Victorian home. He turned on the MP3 player at his waist and got ready for his three-mile jog before church.

As he ran this morning, however, the inspirational music he was listening to was just background sound for his thoughts of Aimee Blake. His strong attraction to her surprised him. At times, Jacob wished that he had a steady girlfriend, but past experience had left him with a slew of emotional scars. He had dated Megan Russell all during high school. He'd loved her and thought she loved him, but she'd betrayed him with another man in their senior year. And she wouldn't even tell him who the other man was. The pain ran so deep that he couldn't forget it, and he didn't want to get involved again. He dated occasionally but always avoided becoming serious about anyone.

He wasn't sure that would be true with Aimee. Already, he was looking forward to speaking to her on the phone and seeing her again. He definitely didn't want a serious relationship, so why was he thinking about her? If, after two brief meetings, he was eager to see Aimee, maybe it would be better to avoid her completely.

Jacob ran vigorously and, in spite of the mid-thirties' cold, his body was steaming when he came back in sight of the house. He slowed his pace to a slow walk as he reached the front lawn.

A pert robin hopped around the grass, looking for breakfast in the ground. Jacob smiled when he saw a few dandelions beaming their yellow presence in the frosty grass. Although many people disliked dandelions in their lawns, they were such hardy plants that they encouraged him to keep going when the way was difficult.

Before he went to his apartment over the garage, Jacob stepped inside the house to check on his grandmother. Looking at her small frame, gray hair and the many wrinkles lining her face, he knew some might consider her an old woman. But the depth of her spiritual faith and her good health belied her seventy-plus years and made Stella one of the most powerful women Jacob knew.

"A nice morning for a run," Gran commented. "How did the singles meeting go last night?"

"Very well," he said. "The program was good, and Erica brought her neighbor, Aimee Blake, to the meeting. She seemed to enjoy it, and she may be interested in helping us with Siblings. I'm going to contact her about it."

"I've heard Erica talk about a neighbor she's wanted to bring to the singles meeting. She's a widow, I believe?"

"That's the one. She has one daughter who's fourteen. We didn't talk long, but I gathered Aimee was sincerely interested in our work."

"We can use her help at the office," Gran said. "A woman from Social Services called today, and they have two sisters they'd like us to lend a hand until they can find foster parents for them. It takes a lot of time to prepare profiles on new applicants, so I can use assistance. Besides, we have more children needing aid than we have volunteers."

"I'll contact Aimee sometime this weekend, and ask her to attend the Siblings meeting Tuesday evening."

Although he wanted to see Aimee again, every time he started to dial her number that morning, Jacob got cold feet and backed out. Badly disillusioned by his fiancée when he was barely out of his teens, he had determined not to go beyond friendship with any woman again.

If she joined the singles group, he would see her monthly, but if he saw her more often in the Siblings meetings, his attraction might grow. He had a feeling Aimee was different from the other women he'd dated. Or was she? He hadn't reached a conclusion before he left for church that morning.

Intent on his job as an usher greeting parishioners and visitors and finding convenient seats for them, Jacob returned to the foyer just as Aimee opened the door and stepped inside. She looked a little lost until she saw him. A smile relaxed her face, and he wondered if she was aware of the enchanting picture she made when she smiled. He noted how the cobalt blouse she wore with a black suit brought out the blue of her eyes. She carried a silver bag, and large silver hoops dangled from her earlobes.

Completely disregarding his intentions to stay a safe distance from Aimee, Jacob hurried toward her with a smile. She returned his smile and accepted the hand he offered.

"Is this becoming a habit?" he said. "We keep running into each other."

"I'm not following you," she said with a low laugh. "I promise."

He took a bulletin from a rack and gave it to her. "Well, it's great that you're here. Let me find a good seat for you."

"Thanks, but I'm meeting Erica. I'll wait for her."

He indicated a row of chairs near the doors to the sanctuary. "Sit there. Erica usually arrives early, so she'll be here soon."

* * *

Aimee glanced through the bulletin as she waited for Erica, surreptitiously watching Jacob as he carried out his assigned duties as usher. His voice was compassionate. He was gracious to old and young alike. She noticed again how captivatingly handsome he was, and decided that Jacob's nature matched his appearance.

Was it just coincidence, or was it significant that she had encountered Jacob three times in as many days? Her granny always used the expression "It was meant to be." Could that be true of her meetings with Jacob? Not that she expected anything from him, but she could use another friend right now.

Her attention was diverted from Jacob when Erica hurried into the foyer. Aimee felt her face warming when Erica caught her intense scrutiny of the man. Jacob would have escorted them to a seat, but Erica waved him aside.

"Why didn't you tell me Jacob would be at this service?" Aimee said as they walked down the aisle.

"I didn't think about it."

"He must be a busy man. If he's active here at the church, has a counseling business and manages Substitute Siblings."

"He's busy all the time. Sometimes I think he's a man driven to prove himself. He rarely misses a service. Neither does his grandmother, Stella Milton. If I see her, I'll introduce you to her. You'll like her."

"This is a *big* room," Aimee commented as they walked to the front of the long, formal sanctuary. They faced a pulpit several feet above the main floor, with a wide spread of organ pipes as a backdrop. A praise band was gathering to lead the opening service. The communion table featured an arrangement of white lilies behind an open Bible.

"The room is full most of the time. Where's Samantha? Wouldn't she come with you?"

Aimee answered, "I didn't ask her. She came upstairs and announced that she was going to the mall with Jennifer. Instead of arguing, I told her that was good so she wouldn't be alone while I went to church."

"She looked as if she thought I'd lost it, but she didn't say anything. It's obvious she doesn't want to be with me, yet she doesn't want me to go anywhere without her either. Rather ironic, isn't it?"

The service felt a little like coming home. It was a familiar blend of hymns, prayer, Bible reading and a sermon. The minister gave a powerful sermon on the text "Choose You This Day Whom You Will Serve?" Now that she had recommitted to a closer walk with God, Joshua's words when he called the Hebrews to repentance held particular significance for Aimee. Before the service was over, she realized how good it was to be worshiping with God's people again.

Aimee didn't see Jacob as she left the service. She felt a slight hurry to face Samantha and stop putting off the inevitable. She prayed for guidance on how to approach her daughter when she got home, for she didn't want to antagonize Samantha and cause her to be even more rebellious. But as a parent, she was responsible for guiding her daughter toward maturity and hoped to reestablish a loving connection.

She drew a deep breath when she heard Samantha enter the house. Sam was carrying a bag from one of the shoe stores in the mall. No doubt she'd been spending some of the birthday money her grandparents in Florida had sent her.

"Hi, Mom," Samantha said, and quickly turned to go to her room.

"Come in here for a moment, please."

Samantha paused on the threshold. "Why?"

"We need to talk," Aimee said, and Samantha's eyes narrowed a bit. Still holding her package, Samantha flounced down on the couch opposite Aimee's chair.

Drawing a deep breath, Aimee said, "I've done

a lot of thinking since you left for Jennifer's sleep-over yesterday. I've concluded that I haven't been a good mother to you."

Samantha's gray eyes, so much like her father's, opened in surprise. "What do you mean?"

"Well," Aimee said, "I've given you too much attention, too much love, too much freedom to choose your friends and make other personal decisions. Lately, you've been acting self-centered and disrespectful, at least to me, although I hope you show respect to other adults. Starting today, that has to change."

"What does that mean?" Samantha's eyes studied her mother pointedly.

"For starters," Aimee answered, "from now on I expect you to assume some household chores, at least to clean your room and make your bed. And *I'm* taking you to school and picking you up as I've always done. When our relationship is better, we'll talk again about you riding to school with Jennifer."

Speechless for a few seconds, Samantha finally said, "You're kidding, right?"

Shaking her head decisively, Aimee said, "I've never been more serious in my life."

"Mom, when can I have a life? Stop treating me like a baby." Samantha stared at her mother as if she were a monster.

"I've given you more freedom than I should have, and I'm not sure that was a good thing. I also had a call from your math teacher, and I didn't like her report. Your grades need to improve overall. If you don't carry a B average the rest of the year, you may have to take classes this summer."

"That isn't fair!"

"Perhaps not, but that's the way it will be."

"I'll tell Grammy!"

"I'm sure you will, but Grandmother Blake isn't your mother. She doesn't get to decide what you do. Besides, I don't think she would interfere in my decisions anyway."

The phone rang, putting their discussion on hold as Samantha bounced out of the chair and ran to answer.

She soon returned and handed the cordless phone to Aimee. "It's for you."

"Who is it?" Aimee asked, thinking if it was Erica, she'd return her call later.

"I don't know."

Aimee sighed with exasperation. "Hello."

"Aimee, this is Jacob Mallory. I had some information about our Siblings program in my car this morning that I meant to give you, but somehow I missed seeing you leave."

"Erica and I left through the side entrance."

"If you tell me where you live," Jacob said, "I'll drop it off at your house this evening. Or I have another suggestion—there's a meeting of Siblings directors and volunteers Tuesday night. We'll be discussing plans for the future. If you'll attend, you could get an idea of what we do and meet the people you'd be working with if you decide to join us. I'll pick you up if you want to go."

Aware that Samantha was staring at her accusingly, Aimee deliberated slightly before she said, "I'd like to go to the meeting, and it would be great if you'd stop by for me. We live at 305 Simpson Place."

"I'll pick you up at half past six. Will that work?"

"That would be fine. See you then," Aimee said and hung up the phone. To Aimee's surprise, Samantha didn't demand to know who had called, so Aimee didn't comment on the belligerence reflected in her daughter's eyes.

"That was Jacob Mallory," she explained. "I met him at the meeting Friday night."

"And you're already going on a date with him?"

"It isn't a date," Aimee explained. "He's invited me to a meeting to learn more about Substitute Siblings, a volunteer organization he and his grandmother founded."

Samantha's eyebrows lowered in an angry

frown. "Is that the group who looks after orphans and street kids?"

"I understand that's part of their work," Aimee said.

"Mom!" Samantha shrieked. "If you have anything to do with them, everybody at school will make fun of me. How can you treat me like this? You're so mean!"

Samantha ran to her room sobbing. Aimee jumped up and started to follow, but at the top of the stairs, she stopped abruptly. If she gave in to Samantha's demands now, she might as well forget steering her daughter in a different direction. Although it was one of the hardest things she'd ever done, Aimee turned a deaf ear to her daughter's theatrical sobs, went to her own room and shut the door.

Chapter Four

A robin that seemed to be singing from her windowsill woke Aimee the next morning. She lifted her head and through bleary eyes looked at the clock. Suddenly wide awake, she threw back the blanket, put on her robe and hurried to the head of the stairs.

"Samantha," she called. "Get up. The alarm clock didn't go off. We leave for school in thirty minutes."

"I'm not going! I'm sick."

Startled, Aimee lifted the bottom of her robe and hurried downstairs. Samantha's door was open, and Aimee went in without knocking. Samantha was lying on a stack of pillows, a pitiful look on her face. Her eyes were swollen, and she was sniffing as if she had a cold.

Aimee got a thermometer from the adjacent bathroom cabinet and took her temperature. It was normal. So was her pulse rate.

"Stick out your tongue," Aimee said. Samantha closed her eyes and complied.

Observing her daughter carefully, Aimee wondered if this was a stunt to get sympathy. If Samantha had been crying, that would account for the red eyes and stuffy nose.

"It's too late for me call in to stay home with you. Erica isn't working today, so I'll ask her to check on you a few times. And I'll call during my lunch break. You know, if you're too sick for school today, you're too sick to stay after school and cheer in the game."

Samantha's glare was almost more than Aimee could stand, but she turned away quickly. While Aimee dressed she heard the water running in Samantha's bathroom, and when Aimee was ready, Samantha was standing beside the door, fully dressed, with her backpack over her back.

"Feeling better?"

"A little," Samantha said weakly. "I remembered a science test today. Better not miss it. And the squad is expecting me to be there to do our new routine."

Aimee's heart was a little lighter when Samantha meekly followed her out to the garage, slid into the car and fastened her seat belt. She had wondered more than once what she would do if Jennifer showed up to take Aimee to school. Perhaps the crisis was over. But when Samantha was silent on the way to school and got out of the car without saying goodbye, Aimee knew that although she won the first battle, the war wasn't over yet.

Throughout the day, as she answered the phone, worked at the computer and handed out school supplies to the kids, Aimee's thoughts kept shifting from Samantha's rebellion to Jacob. She hadn't been attracted to any other man for years, so what was it about Jacob that piqued her interest? Maybe he wasn't any different from any other man she'd encountered in the past dozen years; maybe *she* had changed. It was a startling thought.

After Aimee watched Samantha cheer on her team at the game, they made their way home. Samantha stayed in her room all evening, speaking only in monosyllables when Aimee asked questions. Tuesday morning, she was silent also. After school, however, Samantha replied amicably to Aimee's questions about her day. Aimee soon found out the reason for the attitude change.

"Mom, Mrs. Nibert asked me to go with her and Jen to a spring fashion show at the mall tonight. Can I go?"

"What time?"

"About six. She wants to treat us to Chinese before the show."

Aimee deliberated momentarily. That meant she would be home when Samantha left to be certain that Jennifer's mother *was* with them. She felt guilty about not trusting Samantha, but she wouldn't be comfortable at the Siblings meeting unless she knew that the girls weren't alone.

"I guess that will be all right if you get your homework done in the next two hours. You really need to get that math grade up."

Samantha didn't answer, just went to her room immediately. Aimee didn't hear any phone conversations, so she gave Samantha the benefit of the doubt that she was actually studying.

When the Niberts arrived, Aimee walked outside to greet them. "Thanks for taking Samantha. Do you know what time you will be back? I'm going out for the evening, and I don't want Samantha coming home to an empty house."

"I'm not sure," Mrs. Nibert said, "but if you aren't here, we'll stay until you come home."

Aimee thanked her, waved them on their way and turned toward the house. She didn't really know the Niberts well, but she had to give Samantha some space. If fourteen years of parental guidance hadn't taught her daughter the difference between right and wrong, she had failed as a mother. It was time to have some interests of her own, and she turned her thoughts to the evening with Jacob.

By the time Aimee was dressed, she was so nervous, she couldn't sit still. While she paced the floor, she thought about how she felt the first time she had a date with Steve. Because she was only sixteen at the time and he was eighteen, her parents threw a fit when Steve asked her to go out with him. But she had known Steve forever, so in the end they trusted him. It wasn't quite the same as going out with Jacob, who was almost a stranger.

She didn't know why she was worried. Jacob seemed to have a knack of putting people at ease that must come from his profession as a counselor. Besides, she was only going to learn more about Substitute Siblings, right? This was definitely not a date. She just wished someone would tell that to her racing heart.

It had been a long time since Jacob had looked forward to anything as much as he did the evening with Aimee. As he drove the few miles to her house, he thought of the past few years when his only emotional outlet had been his clients and their problems. It had been a blessing when he had organized Substitute Siblings, for it kept his mind occupied with the needs of others rather than his own personal life—or lack of it.

But no matter how many unfortunate children he helped, a part of his heart still seemed empty and unfulfilled. Was it time for him to trust someone again? Would Aimee be the woman he could finally allow into his life—and his heart?

Benton, Virginia, was a town of fifteen thousand, established two hundred years ago in the foothills of the Blue Ridge Mountains. He knew the town so well that he easily maneuvered through the narrow streets as he went to pick her up. Although he hadn't been in the subdivision where Aimee lived, Jacob drove directly to her house without any problem.

He parked along the curb and went to the front door. Aimee soon answered his knock.

She was as pretty as he remembered. As they walked down the sidewalk, he quietly surveyed her. Jacob had a knack for reading people's thoughts, but Aimee was an enigma to him. He had no idea if she was excited about their evening together. Although thoughts of her kept intruding into his mind, he wondered if she had thought about him at all.

Jacob held open the door of his SUV for her, rounded the front of the vehicle and was in the seat beside her before she had her seat belt fastened. "I haven't been in this subdivision before. Have you lived here long?"

"About fourteen years. My husband had a job

in Washington, D.C., but after he died, I didn't want to stay there. My parents live a few miles out in the country from Benton, and I came home to raise Samantha with the support of my family."

He sensed that she was hesitant to talk about her husband, but he asked one more question, "Does your husband's family live here?"

"Only a few cousins. His parents live year-round in Florida, as does my brother-in-law's family. Samantha always spends two weeks with them during the summer. Occasionally, both of us go to Florida for Christmas."

Although there were many more things Jacob wanted to know about Aimee, he would take his time. She'd already indicated that she devoted all of her time to her job and Samantha. Did that mean she hadn't dated at all since she became a widow? Was she still mourning her husband?

Although he wanted to know more about Aimee, he didn't want to pry. During the short drive to his offices, where the meeting would be held, they shifted the conversation to upcoming events in Benton, especially the city's bicentennial celebration to be held in the summer.

"I'm on the planning committee, and we've had to revise our plans this month," Jacob said. "David Harwood, one of the longtime educators in Benton, died a few weeks ago. The committee has decided to honor him at the celebration, so we're changing our schedule to include him. Did you know Mr. Harwood?"

"No, but I've seen him on television several times," Aimee answered. "I heard about his funeral on the evening news. Apparently he had a great influence on the schools and educational program in Benton."

"That's true. He taught at Paramount High School where I attended, but he moved on to administrative positions soon after I graduated. The committee asked me to prepare and deliver a eulogy about him at the bicentennial, but I can't add anything more to my schedule. So they've asked a former resident who lives in Richmond to do it."

Aimee smiled at him. "It seems to me that you do have about all you can do now. Your counseling business, Substitute Siblings, the singles group and church commitments must take up all of your time."

"Just about," he admitted with a laugh. "But I want to keep busy. I suppose I could have found time to write the eulogy, but I didn't think I was qualified to do it. Mr. Harwood came to Paramount High in my senior year, but I wasn't in any of his classes. I was away from Benton for several years, and we seldom met after I moved back home. I didn't know him well enough to speak about him."

Jacob drove into the parking lot adjacent to his two-story, brick building. It was located in an industrial park with many other office buildings and a few factories. Surrounded by a brick wall, they entered through a security gate. Aimee had rarely been in this section of town and had no idea that so many corporations were located in the area. She was quietly thinking about how narrow her life had been as they took an elevator to the second floor of his building and walked down a hallway to a conference room where the meeting was to be held.

Approximately two dozen people were in the room, and Jacob touched Aimee's arm and steered her toward the front where a small woman with short, iron-gray hair was talking with two men.

"Excuse me," Jacob said. "We have a guest tonight." He introduced Aimee to the two men, whose names she promptly forgot. Then he turned to the woman. "Gran, this is Aimee Blake." His eyes softened with obvious fondness for his grandmother as he turned to Aimee. "I want you to meet Stella Milton."

As they shook hands, Aimee quickly assessed Stella. The makeup on her wrinkled face had been skillfully applied. She wore diamond earrings, and her blue suit was trendy. Her dark eyes glowed with intelligence and warmth as she greeted their guest. Aimee judged that she was in her seventies.

Taking Aimee's arm, Stella said, "Come and meet our volunteers."

Stella explained that this was a regularly scheduled monthly meeting, and the first part of the meeting consisted mostly of reports. Although it seemed to be routine stuff, Aimee got a fair idea of what the Siblings volunteers really did. More than thirty children had been contacted in a month's time. The children had been taken on shopping trips, to ball games and movies, or out to eat at their favorite restaurants. The Siblings children as a group had been taken to the circus at the civic center. She gathered that, for the most part, volunteers supplied the finances for these extras, as well as their time. Well, that wouldn't be an issue with her. Although she didn't consider herself wealthy, Aimee was thankful she had an adequate income.

During new business, plans were made for a Fun in the Sun Day at Pioneer Park, an outing for youth enrolled in the Siblings program and their parents. Jacob reported that two of the restaurants in the city had volunteered to provide food and drink. Before she knew it, Aimee had been paired with Jacob to plan entertainment for the youth who didn't want to participate in contact sports.

After the meeting ended, Jacob guided Aimee on a tour of the building. In addition to the conference room, there were three rooms on the second floor, one of which was the Siblings main office, plus his business offices on the first floor. He pointed out a waiting area, the receptionist's office, his consulting room, a small lounge and a snack room.

"I'm impressed," Aimee said as Jacob locked the door and they walked to the car. "Not only by the work of Siblings, but also with the scope of your counseling service."

"I feel that God has really blessed me to become so well established in such a short time. Since I was a child, I wanted to meet the needs of others, but I didn't think I had the ability to enter the medical profession. Counseling seemed to be the right outlet I needed to fulfill what God created me to do."

Jacob waved to the security guard as they drove from the parking lot.

"Your grandmother seems like a lovely person," Aimee commented.

"She is. Everybody loves Gran."

"What about your parents?" Aimee asked. "Do they live in Benton?"

The streetlights illuminated the interior of the SUV, and Aimee watched Jacob's expressive face go blank. His jaw tightened and his eyes darkened with emotion.

Automatically, she stretched her hand toward him. "Oh, I'm sorry I asked. I had no right. Please forgive me."

From what she had seen of Jacob Mallory, she wouldn't have dreamed that there were any dark areas of his life that he couldn't, or didn't want to, reveal.

He took her hand and squeezed it gently. When he glanced toward her, the pain was gone from his eyes, and he smiled, but not as brightly as usual.

"Of course you have the right to ask. You've answered the questions I've asked about your family." Still he hesitated, and finally said in a husky voice. "I assume I have a father somewhere, although I've never known him. He abandoned my mother when I was less than a year old. They married when they were students at the University of Pennsylvania, and I was born a year later. He hung around for a few months, but apparently he wasn't ready for family responsibilities. He left one day and, as far as I know, she never heard from him again."

"I'm so sorry," Aimee said.

Now that he'd started talking, it seemed easier for Jacob, but still his voice was distant as he continued. "Mother never got over his rejection.

She died when I was six years old from a severe case of pneumonia and flu, but she'd been dying inside since he left her. She didn't handle rejection very well, and I guess I don't either," he ended, almost in a whisper. Then he added, "Gran had most of the care of me while my mother lived, and she gave me all of the love I needed. I had a happy childhood, but I suppose all guys miss their dad."

Up until now, Jacob had appeared to be without any problems. Maybe this was the reason he had chosen to become a counselor? He wanted to deal with his own hang-ups as well as the problems of his clients.

"So by not trying to get well," Aimee asked quietly, "do you feel as if your mother rejected you, too?"

A look of surprise swept over Jacob's face, and he replied thoughtfully, "Maybe so, although I hadn't really thought of it before." He laughed, and the tense moment seemed to have passed. "Aimee, you should have been the counselor."

"I doubt that I would have succeeded in that profession," Aimee replied with a chuckle. "It's difficult enough to deal with one adolescent daughter."

When they stopped in front of her house, Aimee put her hand on Jacob's arm. "Again, I'm sorry for prying, but as for your life with your grandmother, she did a great job in raising you, as far as I can tell. I don't believe you missed much."

"Thanks. I'm trying to be a credit to her. After all Gran has done for me, I don't want to let her down."

"Samantha isn't home yet," Aimee said, "so we're here in plenty of time. Thanks for asking me to the meeting."

He got out of the car and opened the door for her. As they walked toward the house, he asked, "Is it too soon to know if you're willing to be a Siblings volunteer?"

"Yes," Aimee said. "I'll have to think about it and see how I can fit it into my schedule. Maybe there's work I can do at home until school is out. I could probably help more during the summer break. But I'll find time to help with Fun in the Sun. I miss not doing things like that with Samantha."

She took the house key from her purse, opened the door and invited, "Would you like to come in and meet Samantha when she gets here?"

He shook his head. "I'd like to, but I have some computer work to complete tonight. Is it okay for me to call you?"

"Yes, of course."

Jacob's gaze traveled over her face and searched her eyes, suddenly causing a stirring of her heart she hadn't experienced for a long time. He bent toward her until she felt his warm breath on her face, and her pulse tingled at the thought that he was going to kiss her. Suddenly, he shook his head and stepped back.

"Good night, Aimee. I'll be in touch in a few days and we can make plans for Fun in the Sun."

Slightly disappointed, Aimee went inside and watched from the dark hallway as Jacob drove away. What had happened to her common sense since she'd met Jacob Mallory? She wasn't sure it was a good idea to start a relationship now, when Samantha was already testing the waters as an adolescent. It would probably be better to wait a few years, until Samantha was safely off to college. But Aimee wondered, if she waited, would she be losing her only chance of finding a new life—and a new love?

Chapter Five

Jacob had attempted to hide his distress so that Aimee wouldn't feel bad about saying the wrong thing to him, but as soon as he drove away from her house, reaction set in. A few blocks from her house, he pulled over to the curb, stopped the vehicle and slouched over the steering wheel.

His resentment of his absent father was one of the hardest situations he faced in living a Christian life. And when this resentment surfaced, he didn't even feel as if he was a good counselor. How could he counsel clients who had a grudge toward family members when he knew he hadn't forgiven his father for abandoning him? He'd prayed often for the grace to forgive his father, so why couldn't he put it behind him?

Aware of how his father's abandonment concerned Jacob, several times Gran had suggested that he search for his father. The last time the subject was mentioned, Gran had said, "For all you know, your father may be dead, or perhaps he was involved in a situation that made it impossible for him to contact you."

"Well, if that's the case, there isn't any need to search," Jacob had replied.

"But you're certain to have other relatives. Perhaps grandparents, aunts, uncles and cousins," Gran had quietly insisted.

"I don't even know where his family lived. If only Mother had told me more about him before she died. I think I remember asking her questions a few times, but she ignored me. She could have at least told me that."

As Jacob pulled back onto the road and headed home, he realized that he resented his mother's silence even more than his father's desertion. She should have leveled with him about the trouble between her and his father.

And as he thought of their conversation, Jacob knew that Aimee had a point. He did have hard feelings toward his mother, too. He resented his father for abandoning him and his mother, and he blamed her for dying before he was old enough for her to answer some of his questions. He drove into the garage, turned off the engine and leaned his head on the steering wheel.

"God," he moaned in distress, *"I can't carry this burden much longer. Give me some guidance. This is ruining my life."*

Jacob had almost kissed her. Why did he draw back? Aimee was alarmed at her own reaction. She'd *wanted* him to kiss her! What had happened to her? A week ago she was perfectly satisfied with her life. Now, it seemed like everything had gone haywire.

She had been content to live out her life as a mother, eventually a mother-in-law and a grandmother. Now, after seeing Jacob Mallory a few times, she wondered if that was enough. She finally had to admit to herself that she was lonely. She knew she was no longer satisfied with her life as it was.

As she undressed for bed, Aimee made up her mind that Samantha was still her first responsibility, and always would be. She'd have to be very cautious if there was going to be any room in her life for a friendship with Jacob. Still, as the week passed, Aimee was disappointed when he didn't call, and she wondered if it was already too late to guard her heart.

Although she had intended to return to Memorial Church on Sunday, when she woke up on Saturday with Jacob on her mind, she wondered if she should go. Was he annoyed because she had questioned him about his family? Since he hadn't called, she guessed he didn't want to see her. Or did he think she was expecting more from him than he was willing to give? If he was interested in her only as a possible volunteer for Substitute Siblings, she didn't want him to assume she was pursuing him by showing up at places where she knew he would be.

So on Saturday afternoon when Erica called and invited her to ride to church with her the next morning, Aimee turned her down. "I haven't visited my folks for a few weeks, so I'm going to see them tomorrow. I'll go to their church. That will make them happy. They haven't approved of the way I've neglected worship."

When Samantha came upstairs for dinner, Aimee said, "How about going to see Papaw and Grammy tomorrow?"

"All right, I guess," Samantha said.

"Let's leave early enough to go to church with them."

"Hey, what's up, Mom? Why are you pushing church at me all of a sudden?"

Aimee felt her face flushing. It was hard for her to come up with the words to explain to Samantha about the time she'd spent with God a few nights ago. But she had to let Samantha know that she intended to follow the teachings of the Bible more closely in the future than she'd been doing for several years.

"I told you a few days ago that I haven't been a very good mother. One of the things I've neglected is your spiritual life. I want you to understand that God is real, that He loves you, and that He wants a relationship with you—and with me."

Samantha stared at Aimee for a few seconds and then lowered her head, seemingly embarrassed.

"I'm going to attend Sunday worship regularly from now on," Aimee stated, "and I intend for you to go with me."

Samantha stirred uneasily in her chair, chewed on her lower lip and said hesitantly, "Mmm, I'll go with you tomorrow. But no promises about next time."

"It isn't a matter of promising—it's called parental responsibility. When I haven't been attending worship, I didn't expect you to go without me. Now I realize that I've been wrong. Spiritual growth is just as important for a mother to promote as seeing that you have the proper food to grow physically."

"Aw, Mom, do we have to talk about this now? I've got tons of things to do." Samantha started toward her room.

"Please sit down and listen to me," Aimee said. "If you were skipping classes at school, for your own good I'd see that you stopped that. It's just as important for you to have spiritual training. I expect you to start going to Sunday worship."

Samantha studied her mother's face momentarily, as if wondering if she could change her mind. Apparently, she decided she couldn't.

"Okay, I'll go, but I won't like it."

Aimee nodded. "I'll call Mom and Dad and tell them we'll be there tomorrow."

As Jacob went about his work, exercises and private meditations all week, Aimee often intruded into his thoughts. Several times he started to punch in the digits of her phone number, only to lay the phone aside. He kept hoping she would call him first, perhaps to discuss their participation in Fun in the Sun Day. As the days passed, he decided she wasn't interested in him.

But as the weekend approached, he remembered that Aimee had indicated she would come to church again. When Sunday morning came, he headed to the church with enthusiasm and hope. When Erica came into the foyer and Aimee wasn't with her, his spirits plummeted. He didn't ask Erica why Aimee hadn't come. If he asked about Aimee, she would probably read too much into his question. He found himself distracted during the service wondering why she wasn't there.

On his way home, Jacob decided he was acting

like a teenager, rather than a man who'd been making relatively intelligent decisions for several years. Because Aimee was a widow with a teenager to raise, he knew she had a lot of difficult decisions to make in regards to her daughter. They should probably just be friends for a while. Right? They could be friends, and friends call to see how their friend is doing. He felt as if a burden had been lifted from his shoulders, and as he pulled into the driveway, he took out his cell and dialed her number, anticipating her pleasant, lilting voice.

He felt like a deflated balloon when he got her answering machine. "You've reached the home of Aimee and Samantha Blake. Leave a message, please."

So sure that he would reach her, Jacob was at a loss for words. He considered disconnecting without saying anything, but if Aimee had caller ID, she would see that he'd called.

"This is Jacob Mallory," he said at last. "I missed you at church this morning. Talk to you later."

He disconnected, wondering if he had used the right approach. He hadn't asked her to return his call, so if she didn't want to see him again, she wouldn't call back. *Please, God, let her call back.*

Aimee's pleasant day with her parents lifted her spirits considerably. Ed Ross had been the mail carrier for thirty years on a rural route out of Benton, and her parents lived on a small farm about a forty-five-minute drive from Aimee's house.

Papaw and Samantha went fishing in the afternoon. While her mother knitted an afghan, Aimee relaxed on the couch. For some reason, she was in a nostalgic mood, and she turned the conversation toward the past, mentioning some of the good times she'd enjoyed with her parents, wondering if she had provided enough pleasant memories so that she and Samantha would some day reminisce like this. All in all, it had been a good day.

The light on the answering machine was blinking when they entered the family room, and Samantha rushed to pick up the message while Aimee took off her coat and hung it up. She had started toward her bedroom when she heard Jacob's voice. She turned quickly into the family room. Samantha stood staring at the phone and turned to her mother as Aimee hit the replay button.

Aimee's spirits soared as she listened. "This is Jacob Mallory. I missed you at church this morning. Talk to you later."

Although she told herself it was nonsense to get so much satisfaction from a voice mail, she couldn't deny the ripple of excitement that went through her at the sound of his voice. When the message ended, she pushed the stop button and turned to face her daughter, who had a suspicious look in her eyes.

"Jacob Mallory again?" Samantha exclaimed. "Do you like him, Mom?"

"I don't know. As a friend. I'll be seeing him some over the next few weeks. I'm helping him with a Siblings outing at Pioneer Park. We could use your help, too."

"You've got to be kidding," Samantha said disgustedly. "Are you going to call him back?"

Aimee shrugged. "Probably, but not right now."

Samantha tossed her head defiantly and ran downstairs.

When Aimee heard the bedroom door slam, she knew that their friendly day had been only a reprieve. Although she wanted to return Jacob's call, if she had to choose between his friendship and her daughter, there could be only one choice. Samantha.

But her heart didn't seem to agree. If she didn't return his call, she was convinced Jacob wouldn't contact her again. Aimee felt sure that he was interested in her, but if Erica said he only dated women casually, she needed to go slow. Since Jacob had been rejected by both his father and mother, it was obvious to Aimee now that he couldn't open himself to similar treatment by a woman. Still, if she allowed Samantha to call the shots on the issue of Aimee even making friends, she would try the same tactics again and again. Her daughter wouldn't control her if Aimee could help it, so she decided to return Jacob's call.

Since Samantha could easily listen in on their conversation if she used the house phone, Aimee went to the bedroom and picked up her cell. She found Jacob's home number on the business card he'd given her at the Siblings meeting, kicked off her shoes and lounged on the bed before she punched it in.

Jacob answered on the second ring.

"Hi, Jacob. This is Aimee, returning your call."

"Thanks for calling back," he said, and she thought she detected his pleasure at her call. "I missed seeing you at church this morning."

"Samantha and I visited my parents today, and we went to church with them. They live a few miles out of town. We haven't been home very long."

"Is your dad a farmer?"

Laughing a bit, Aimee says, "He plays at being a farmer. They own about forty acres that belonged to my maternal grandparents. He was a rural mail carrier for years, and he rented the farmland then. When he retired, he bought some farming machinery and a few cattle, and he spends his time puttering around on the farm."

Aimee wondered if she was babbling too much about her happy family when Jacob obviously hadn't had one. She quickly changed the subject. "How's your grandmother?"

"Keeping busy as usual!" he responded, and she imagined a smile crossing his face. He obviously doted on his grandmother. "I hope I have that much energy when I'm her age. We have several new children eligible for adult mentoring, so she's been trying to match them with a willing person."

"I'm still planning to help with Fun in the Sun, but I feel that I should do more. Until school's out, I can't help Stella in the office, but I might be able to entertain someone on Saturdays. How often would I need to contact the child?"

"That's up to you. As I said before, most of our children aren't orphans, but for various reasons, they need some extra attention," Jacob explained. "What you do can be as simple as calling on the phone, taking a child to a movie, inviting her to your home to bake cookies or taking her shopping. It depends on the age and situation of the child, as well as what the adult is able to give. Since you have a daughter, it would probably be natural for you to befriend a teenage girl."

"I'll think about it," Samantha said.

Jacob didn't respond, and she continued, "Well, I'd better stop talking and prepare for tomorrow. Mondays are not the best days at school—too many cranky kids and tired teachers who've tried to do a week's work in two days. Thanks again for calling. I'll plan to be at church next Sunday."

"I'd like to see you before then, if possible," Jacob said slowly. "Do you have *any* free time?"

Aimee's heart skipped a beat. "Not until the weekend, and maybe not even then. I think Saturday is the date for Samantha's cheerleading squad to have a car wash to raise money. The parents usually go along."

"Maybe another time, then."

Aimee sensed his disappointment, or was it only an echo from her own heart? Although she didn't know how deep her interest in Jacob was, she did want to explore the growing feelings she was developing for him.

"Actually, I'm home most weeknights," she reconsidered. "As soon as dinner is over, Samantha usually goes to her room, and I'm basically alone. If you want, you're welcome to stop by some night. That would give us an opportunity to make plans for Fun in the Sun activities."

"Count on it," Jacob responded with added warmth in his voice. "Tuesday looks like a good time, but I'll call you to make sure."

After she hung up, Aimee laid the phone aside and covered her face with her hands while a jumble of confused thoughts and feelings tumbled over her. Was it a mistake to invite Jacob to her home? What would Samantha read into that invitation?

After she undressed and prepared for the night, Aimee sat in her lounge chair, extended the footrest, leaned back and closed her eyes.

Four years from now, Samantha would graduate from high school and be ready for college, and she might choose to go to school in Florida near Steve's family. If that happened, Aimee would be alone for the first time in eighteen years.

She had guided Samantha's life the best she knew how, but she could see that it was time now to prepare for her *own* future. If the house seemed quiet when Samantha was away overnight, what would it be like when she was gone for months?

Aimee was tired, but the way her thoughts were racing, she knew she wouldn't be able to sleep. She picked up Steve's Bible from the nightstand, knowing that the answer to any problem could be found in God's Word. She closed her eyes. *"God,"* she prayed, *"guide me to a scripture that will point me in the right direction. Although I've been Your follower for years, I've not been in close fellowship with You like I should be. I want to change that."*

With her eyes still closed, she turned the pages randomly. She opened her eyes to see that her hands had stopped at the third chapter of the first Book of Kings. Recalling some of the passages she had read in the Old Testament, it seemed an unlikely place to find the answers she looked for. But believing that God had directed her, she shrugged her shoulders and explored each verse in the chapter.

It was part of the story of Solomon, one of the noted kings of the Israelites. Solomon had asked God for wisdom to guide his people, and his wish had been granted.

Perplexed, Aimee whispered, *"But, God, how can I apply this to my own life? I don't have a multitude of people to guide—only one young girl and myself. What are You trying to tell me?"*

She scanned the chapter again, and understanding came when she read the words "So give your servant a discerning heart…to distinguish between right and wrong."

Aimee considered what she had read and understood that she would need to show good judgment in the decisions she made concerning her relationships with Samantha and with Jacob.

"God," she prayed, *"I'll rely on You to give me that understanding. I don't suppose even Solomon made the right call every time. He wouldn't have known in advance the situations he would face, either. So instead of worrying what I should do four years down the road, I just*

*need to take this—with Your help—one day at a
time. Right?"*

As she slipped under the covers and turned out
the light, Aimee's heart was strangely at peace. To
trust God completely, she had to stop worrying
about every move she made. She had to realize
that she wasn't strong enough physically or spiri-
tually to prepare in advance for every situation
that would come up.

It was difficult for Aimee to admit that she
needed help, but she acknowledged the necessity
to depend on God, especially in her relationship
with Jacob. But how would she respond if it was
God's will that she avoid him?

Chapter Six

Since it wasn't definite that Jacob would visit on Tuesday night, Aimee didn't mention it to Samantha. All day long she fought to keep her mind on her work, which wasn't easy, when she considered that their meeting tonight could be a turning point in her budding relationship with the first man she had been attracted to in more than ten years.

The day seemed longer than usual, and it was a relief when she walked out of Eastside Elementary and picked up Samantha at the high school. Samantha's book bag seemed well filled, and when she tossed it on the back seat of the car, Aimee asked, "Lots of homework tonight?"

"More like tons!"

So far, so good, Aimee thought. If Samantha was busy studying, she and Jacob could have some time together.

"I hoped we wouldn't have any work. I wanted to watch the DVD Madison loaned me."

"Maybe you'd better let me keep the DVD so you won't be tempted to watch it."

"Give me a break, Mom."

The look on Samantha's face wasn't encouraging, and although she'd been thinking for two days about seeing Jacob, Aimee now wished he wouldn't call. Was Jacob's company worth added tension with Samantha?

The phone was ringing when they went inside, and thinking it might be Jacob, Aimee picked up the receiver before Samantha could reach it. She was right.

After greeting her, he said, "I'm free for tonight. Is it still all right to come over?"

"Yes, I think so."

"I'll be there about seven, and I'll bring a pizza if you haven't eaten. Cheese or pepperoni?" Jacob said eagerly.

"Whatever you pick would be great. See you then," Aimee responded.

"Who was that?" Samantha demanded when Aimee put the phone back in its cradle.

"Jacob Mallory," Aimee answered. "He's stopping by tonight."

"The one you went out with last week?" Samantha asked suspiciously.

"I only went to a meeting with him," Aimee said. "I don't consider that 'going out.'"

A doubtful expression on her face, Samantha headed to her room. "Fine, then I'll get busy with my homework."

"Come up and meet Jacob when he gets here, please," Aimee said.

"I will, okay?" Samantha answered, but she didn't meet Aimee's eyes before she left the family room.

Jacob's pulse accelerated when he drove into the cul-de-sac where Aimee lived and parked in front of her home. Although he wasn't sure there was room for romance in either of their lives, he had to admit he enjoyed Aimee's company and could see no reason not to be friends. He was glad she had invited him to her home, for he wanted to meet Samantha. He sensed that his friendship with Aimee hinged on her daughter.

He knocked, and Aimee soon opened the door, took the pizza from his hands and invited him inside. Soft, classical music greeted him and seemed to set the mood for their evening. As they walked into a family room adjacent to the kitchen, he saw a formal dining room to the right. A hallway to the left apparently led to the bedrooms of the house.

Although the family room was large, the furniture grouped into small visiting areas made it comfortable and cozy. One section had several upholstered chairs arranged around a television. A desk was located in one corner. A lounge chair stood near a wide bay window, and Jacob's attention was drawn to the small courtyard outside. Landscape stones formed several walkways around a wooden bench and several bird feeders.

"This is nice," he commented as Aimee stood beside him.

"This is my favorite place in the whole house," she said.

"I can see why," Jacob agreed.

"I sit in the courtyard a lot during the summer." She motioned to one of the other chairs. "Please, sit down. Can I bring you some coffee or a cold drink with your pizza?"

"Just ice water would be great." He settled into the chair, and she put the pizza on plates, brought in their drinks and sat down across from him. "You have a comfortable home. I've forgotten how many years you said you've been here?"

"Since Samantha was a baby. The house was new when we moved in."

"Hi, I'm Samantha," Samantha said from the doorway. She held a DVD in her hand. "Is it all right if I hang out with you guys?"

Jacob stood and turned toward Samantha. Aimee sliced a quick glance toward her daughter, who stepped forward with an innocent expression on her face.

She extended her hand to him. "Glad to meet you, Mr. Mallory." She sat down in a chair beside Aimee. "Mom said you were coming over. I've got a DVD to watch—thought I'd share it with you. And is that pizza? Mom, can I have a piece?"

Eyeing Samantha uneasily, Aimee said, "Have you finished your homework?"

"Yep. It didn't take as much time as I thought it would."

Aimee gave Samantha two slices of pizza and poured a glass of cola for her.

"I'm sure Jacob doesn't want to watch the DVD," Aimee said. "You can watch it tomorrow night."

Jacob sensed a heightened tension in the room, and he said, "No, that's fine. It looks like a *Star Wars* movie. I watched them a long time ago."

"Great!" Samantha said, jumping up from her chair and inserting the DVD. "You can sit in this chair. It has a good view of the TV." She pulled a chair between Jacob's and Aimee's and sat in it, holding the plate on her lap.

During the movie, Jacob and Samantha cheered at appropriate places, but Aimee seldom uttered a word. Had he made a mistake in agreeing to watch the DVD? The movie lasted two hours, and by the time it was over, Jacob was miserable, because he knew Aimee was not happy.

"Thanks for sharing the movie with me," he said, standing when Samantha pushed the remote button and turned off the television. "It was, and still is, one of my favorites. But it's a work—and school—night, and I should leave."

Aimee stood, too. With a thin-lipped smile, she said, "Let me wrap up the extra pizza first for you to take with you."

He followed her into the kitchen separated from the family room by a row of base cabinets. Samantha tagged along behind them and sat down at the table.

Jacob wandered around the kitchen while Aimee put the leftover slices in a plastic bag. He stopped beside a photo of a smiling young man on the wall.

"Your husband?" he asked quietly.

"Yes, taken the year he died," she said slowly. "Steve and Samantha look a lot alike, don't they?"

From the tension in the air, it was obvious that Samantha was determined to keep Aimee and him from having any time alone. He felt sorry for Aimee, who paid no attention to Samantha, although the girl continually cast speculative glances toward her mother.

Hesitating to make his departure too abruptly, he asked, "Samantha, how is the school year going for you?"

She shrugged. "Oh, my grades are average except in math, and that's the pits. I've got to keep a C average to still be a cheerleader."

Jacob glanced toward Aimee, but she didn't meet his eyes.

"Do you have a certain profession in mind for when you go to college?"

"Uh, I'm only a freshman, so not yet," Samantha said.

"I'd better go. I have to get up early tomorrow morning. Thanks for the movie and the company."

Aimee accompanied him to the door, with Samantha dogging their steps.

"Nice to meet you, Mr. Mallory," Samantha said.

He almost sighed at the frustration he was experiencing, knowing from the expression on Aimee's face that she felt the same way. He said good-night and walked toward his car. He wondered how Aimee would handle the precocious Samantha. They hadn't even gotten to plan any of the Fun in the Sun activities. At that thought, Jacob brightened. They'd just have to get together again—and soon.

Aimee abruptly closed the door behind Jacob and leaned against it. Samantha headed toward the stairway. "Past bedtime, Mom. See ya in the morning."

"All right, honey. I love you."

Samantha looked ashamed, and she came to Aimee and lifted her face for a good night kiss.

Although she was humiliated and angry about Samantha's obvious efforts to keep her and Jacob apart, Aimee couldn't deal with it tonight.

Samantha had been insolent tonight, and Aimee didn't know what to do. She needed to stop this rebellious attitude of Samantha's without losing her daughter's love and trust. It would take a lot of prayer and love to do that.

What must Jacob think of them? She probably would never know, for she doubted she would ever see Jacob again. She couldn't blame him if he never called. She had looked forward to the evening more than she'd imagined, and it had been ruined. She got into her nightclothes and went to bed, shivering in spite of the warmth of the blankets. Succumbing to a luxury she hadn't enjoyed for a long time, Aimee cried herself to sleep.

The ringing alarm awakened Aimee, and she covered her head with a pillow. She was dreaming of the day she'd learned she was pregnant and how happy Steve had been when she told him. If he had lived, would they still be happy now?

The snooze alarm reminded her that she was still in bed. She struggled to her feet and dressed for the day, wondering how she could possibly work for eight hours.

Samantha waited by the kitchen door when it was time to leave for school. "I fixed your juice and toast, Mom."

"Thanks, sweetie. That was nice of you."

Later, constantly thinking of the impending talk with Samantha, Aimee forced herself to do her work, and she smiled at any of the children who came to the office, but her heart was numb. Somehow she got through the day, and when she picked up Samantha, she managed to ask, "How was your day?" She wanted to act as if last night hadn't happened, but she couldn't. At this point, she felt more like a child than a mother.

She sensed Samantha's covert glances in her direction, and finally she blurted out, "Mom, talk to me. What is it with you? I was just trying to be polite to company."

Yeah, right. So Samantha knew exactly why her mother was angry. Aimee didn't answer because it wouldn't be safe to start an argument with Samantha while she was driving. When they arrived at home, Samantha huffed out of the car.

Aimee followed her into the house and said roughly, "Sit down! I'm ready to talk now."

Samantha slouched into a chair in the family room and looked at the ceiling. Aimee sat opposite her.

"Samantha, why?" Aimee bit her lips to stop their quivering. "Why did you embarrass me the way you did last night?"

"What did I do? I was just being polite to company," Samantha said flippantly.

"You're lying, and you know it. Also, I had a call from your math teacher today, and she told me you didn't do your homework, although you told me you had. You went out of your way to see that Jacob and I didn't spend one minute alone."

"And why does that matter, Mom? What did you want to *do* with him? You said you weren't dating him. You're the one who lied!"

Aimee's self-control almost gave way, and she trembled when she continued, "All of your life you've brought home any friend you wanted, and I've been really good to them. But when *I* invite a friend to the house, you act like someone I don't even know."

"Sorry about that."

Aimee had been holding back tears all day, but she couldn't control them any longer. Samantha stared at her in utter astonishment as tears overflowed her eyes and down her face. No wonder she was surprised. Aimee had been careful to be a happy mom for Samantha. She probably hadn't seen her mother cry before.

Suspecting that she was probably overreacting, Aimee told her daughter they would talk more later, then went to her bedroom and closed the door. *God, help me know what to do here. Help my feelings for Jacob not get in the way of being a good mom. Help me to show Samantha that there is room in my heart for friendships without taking anything away from her. Please heal our relationship, God, and give me wisdom like Solomon.*

With a sigh, Aimee rolled over and went to sleep.

Jacob waited for two days before he called Aimee, hoping that Aimee would answer instead of her daughter.

"Aimee, this is Jacob. How are you?"

She sniffed audibly before saying in a cross voice, "Do you really want to know how I am, or are you just asking to open the conversation?"

Laughing, he said, "To be honest, I'd have to say both."

"Well, first of all, I'm still mad," Aimee snapped. "Mad at myself and mad at Samantha. I'm also embarrassed that she acted as if she thought she had to chaperone us. You probably don't have a good opinion of me as a mother, but truly, I've never known her to be so disrespectful."

"Has she ever had a reason to act that way?" he asked gently.

"I've never invited a male friend to the house before, if that's what you mean."

Jacob's heart skipped a beat. After years of being alone, why had she invited him? Why him and not another man? He filed her comment in his mind to consider later.

"I shouldn't have meddled into your private affairs," he continued, "but that *is* what I meant. Samantha's old enough to realize that you're not only her mother, but also a *woman* as well. I hope you can talk to her and see whether she was just making trouble, or if some part of her is afraid she might lose you if you have other interests."

"You might be right, but my mind is so muddled now I can't deal with any psychology," Aimee said. "I yelled at her, and I need to make peace with her, but it's been too hectic this week to deal with the situation. Thanks for calling. I wouldn't have blamed you if you'd never talked to me again."

"I don't know what else you could have done," Jacob assured her. "You kept trying to catch her eye to warn her, but she carefully avoided looking at you."

Surprised that he'd noticed this, Aimee

replied, "I know. But I couldn't embarrass her before a guest, even it she did act as if I'd never taught her anything."

In a casual way, Jacob suggested, "It may be that Samantha hasn't learned her lesson yet. If you want some free counseling advice, it might be best if you give yourself time to calm down before dealing with it."

"I figure you're right," Aimee said. "I don't know whether I'm feeling anger or disappointment or both, but I don't want to lose control and say things I'll regret. I'll take your advice."

"Actually, I felt a little responsible, too," Jacob admitted, "as if I should have said something. But I didn't want to interfere."

"I appreciate that," Aimee told him. "It *was* my responsibility, but I was so surprised at her behavior that I really didn't know what to do."

"Maybe the best thing is for us to go out when we want to be together, instead of staying at your home," Jacob said. "Could we have dinner together and maybe take in a movie some evening? Or if you don't want to leave Samantha alone at night, we could go out Sunday afternoon."

Aimee deliberated a moment before she said, "Let's plan on an evening. I seldom go out at night because I don't have many outside interests.

But when I have school functions, Samantha is fine on her own until I get home."

"What night would work for you?" Jacob asked.

"Are you free next Monday?"

"Let me check my calendar." He reached in his pocket and checked through his appointment book. "Yes, the night is free."

"Then let's plan on it. I'll let you know if something comes up," Aimee assured him.

"Are you still coming to church on Sunday?" he asked.

"I think so," Aimee said. "And Samantha will be with me."

"I'll save you a seat. See you then." Jacob laid aside the phone, thinking that it would feel like a long time until Monday and wondering again what he was getting himself into.

Would Aimee end up being the woman of his dreams, or was this all going to turn into another long nightmare like the one he'd experienced with his high school sweetheart?

Chapter Seven

Acting on Jacob's advice, Aimee didn't bring up the other evening again. She treated Samantha civilly, and slowly her anger cooled under the weight of Samantha's concerned glances. It was her responsibility as a mother to discipline her daughter without losing control. Aimee loved Samantha dearly, and she hoped her daughter would get out of herself and apologize after a few days of witnessing her mother's hurt.

The rest of the week, while she went about her normal routine, Jacob wasn't far from her mind. How could she avoid thinking about him when he called every night? She could hardly wait for church Sunday and their night out Monday. She shopped on Saturday while Samantha was at Jennifer's and bought a black silk dress with elbow-length sleeves. The gently flared long skirt flowed to her calves, and Aimee felt more feminine than she had for a long time.

Aimee hadn't mentioned church to Samantha since she'd told her the week before that she expected Samantha to go with her. Hoping to avoid further conflict about it, she breathed a silent prayer of thanksgiving when, after they'd finished their dinner Saturday evening, Samantha asked, "Mom, what kind of clothes do I have to wear to church?"

"Any of your casual slacks and shirts will be appropriate," Aimee assured her. "And several of the girls your age wear jeans."

Surprise flitted across Samantha's face. "You mean other girls go to church there?"

Smiling, Aimee said, "Of course. Several teenagers sing in the praise band. People of all ages worship there."

"I figured I'd be the only kid there. What time do I have to be ready?"

Aimee told her and pulled Samantha into a tight hug. "I love you, honey."

"I love you back," Samantha said, and Aimee sensed that they were closer than they had been for several months. Was this a foreshadowing of the future when they would settle their differences as woman-to-woman, rather than as an adult to a child?

Erica stopped by to pick them up the next

morning, which pleased Samantha because she and Erica were good friends. When they arrived at the church, Erica asked Samantha to help her take some groceries to the food pantry, so Aimee entered the foyer alone.

Jacob approached and asked with concern, "No Samantha?"

Smiling, Aimee said, "No, she's here. She didn't argue about coming. She's helping Erica take some items to the annex."

Happiness filled Aimee's heart and they chatted briefly as she waited for Samantha and Erica. Jacob greeted Samantha, expressing his pleasure at seeing her again. He introduced Samantha to another girl just entering the foyer with her parents.

"Come and sit with me and friends," the girl invited.

"Is that okay, Mom?" Samantha asked.

"Sure. We'll find you when the service is over."

As Samantha and the girl hurried away, Aimee turned to Jacob. "Thank you," she said.

Their eyes clung for a brief, breathless moment before she entered the sanctuary with Erica.

Erica hadn't missed the silent greeting between Aimee and Jacob. She slanted an amused look from one to other, but she held her tongue, which Aimee considered a miracle and a departure from

Erica's usual forthright manner. Then, as they walked down the aisle, Erica said, "It may be that you're the one who's going to force Mr. Hard-to-Get out of his shell."

Frowning at her, Aimee looked around quickly to see if anyone was close enough to have overheard Erica's remark.

"Hush! I don't want everyone talking."

Erica whispered, "I'll be quiet now, but I expect some details. Don't forget, I'm the one who introduced you. That should give me some priority treatment."

Aimee hadn't mentioned her dinner date with Jacob to anyone, and she intended to keep it to herself until the next day. Until she could interpret her feelings for him, she didn't want Erica quizzing her.

Once they were seated, Erica turned her attention to the bulletin. She took out several sheets of paper, complaining, "I wish they'd stop putting this stuff in the bulletins. Half of them end up being left in the pews for the custodian to clean up."

"I'm sure they must be of interest to someone," Aimee said. "This one, for instance."

Aimee looked closely at a four-fold brochure with ATTENTION LADIES emblazoned in bold letters across the top. "It's for a women's conference the first weekend in May," she said. "I wonder if I should go."

She pointed to the questions on the front.

Has your life suddenly changed direction?
Is your faith weak?
Do you have conflicting emotions and questions about the future?
Do you want to find God's will for your life?
If your answers to these questions are yes, register for the Spiritual Growth Conference at Camp Serenity the third weekend in May.

The organist's call to worship reached the final crescendo, and the worship leader stepped to the podium, but Erica whispered, "I've only gone once, but it's worth the time and money. I'll go with you if you decide to attend."

"We'll see," Aimee whispered and turned her mind to the service.

After the benediction, when they waited until Samantha joined them, Erica headed for the side entrance, and Aimee made no objection, for she preferred to avoid the foyer and crowds. Besides, Jacob was becoming a distraction to her peace of mind. She'd have time enough with him tomorrow night.

"How'd it go?" Erica asked Samantha when they reached the car.

"Okay. I met some cool kids."

When they got home, Samantha thanked Erica for the ride and hurried into the house.

Erica didn't know that Jacob had visited her last week, and Aimee had been too distressed about what had happened to talk about it. Before she got out of the car, she briefly sketched Samantha's behavior and how she had dealt with it.

"Want some advice?" Erica asked.

"No."

Laughing, Erica said, "That won't stop me from giving some. You *are* doing the right thing for yourself and Samantha to start having your own life. But you should keep reassuring her that she's not losing you."

"I agree, but I need to stand up to her, too," Aimee agreed. "I can already see some change in her. I take most of the blame. I've babied her too much, so I have to change also."

"Neither one of you will change overnight. Take it from a woman who raised two daughters. There will always be something cropping up that you'll have to deal with—even after they're away from home like mine are."

"Just so you're the first to know," Aimee said lightly, "I'll tell you that Jacob and I have a date tomorrow night."

A wide grin spread across Erica's face, only to be replaced by a frown. "But don't read too much into that," she warned. "Remember, he's dated other women, but not for long. I'll feel responsible if he dates you for a few times and then dumps you."

Frowning at her friend, Aimee said, "Give me credit for having some smarts. If Jacob treats me that way, don't you think I'd know I was better off without him?"

"Sure you would." She grimaced. "But I just can't help giving advice."

Erica picked up her Bible, purse and bulletin from the car seat. The leaflet about the spiritual growth conference fell out.

"I hope you'll consider going to this conference with me," Erica said. "This has been a stressful year at work, and I need some time away from the daily grind."

"When do I have to decide?" Aimee asked.

Glancing at the brochure, Erica said, "May 5, so we have to make up our minds this week. The retreat starts the third Friday evening in May with dinner and ends Sunday after breakfast."

"I'll see if Samantha will spend the weekend with Mother and Daddy. She usually doesn't need any urging to go to the farm. If she'll stay with my parents that weekend, I'll attend the conference."

* * *

Since Jacob hadn't indicated where they would eat, Aimee thought she might be overdressed for their dinner date. If Samantha resented her going out with Jacob, she didn't say so, and she didn't come upstairs when he arrived. He was wearing a suit and tie, so Aimee knew her clothes were all right.

"You look fantastic!" he murmured.

"I could return the compliment," she said quietly.

"Are you ready?" he asked.

"Just as soon as I grab a coat."

"I've made reservations at the Pines Restaurant," Jacob said as they left the house. "I hope you like their food. I should have asked what you like."

"I haven't been there, but I've heard it's an excellent place to eat, and I like most foods. When we eat out, it's usually where they sell burgers or hot dogs, so this is a real treat."

The restaurant was located on the first floor of an antebellum home, which in earlier days had been the focal point of a large plantation. The driveway was lined with pine trees, and as Jacob drove slowly into the grounds and into the parking lot, it seemed as if they left the modern world behind them. Twilight was falling and candles shone in all the windows. When they reached the four-columned veranda, the door opened and a smiling hostess, dressed in a gray silk dress with a billowing hoop, opened the door and welcomed them to the restaurant.

"This way," she said and turned from the wide hallway into a large room to the right, which Aimee thought must have been the parlor when the house was a private home. The light from the electric candles in the century-old crystal chandelier cast a warm glow around the room.

After they'd placed their order, Jacob leaned back in his chair and searched her face, a glint of wonder shining from his brilliant dark eyes. His steady gaze discomfited her, and self-consciously, she touched her face and her hair, asking, "Why are you staring? Did I forget makeup or is my hair a mess?"

"Sorry. I didn't realize I was staring," he apologized. "I guess I'm just happy that we have a chance to get better acquainted. I think about you a lot. I'm sure you've had many opportunities, yet you told me that you haven't dated since your husband's death. Maybe I'm getting too personal, but do you mind if I ask why?"

"It's all right to ask, but I don't necessarily have an answer," Aimee replied after a moment's hesitation. *Was she really ready to share her personal experiences with Jacob?* "Since I had to be father and mother both, I took seriously my role as a single parent and devoted all my time to

Samantha. Then, too, Steve had provided a nice income for us through insurance and investments. I think I didn't want to be living at his expense and dating someone else. I suppose the bottom line is that I wasn't interested in dating."

She stopped short of telling him about her fears of sharing the intimacies of marriage. It wasn't something she wanted to tell anyone, certainly not Jacob.

"Apparently you've changed your mind," he said with a grin and a significant lifting of his eyebrows.

"The fact that I'm out with you should be the answer," she said lightly.

"I'm flattered, but I wonder why I'm the lucky guy."

"You know, I sort of wonder, too," Aimee remarked slowly. "I like you, and maybe I just happened to meet you at the right time. Now that Samantha doesn't want me to be involved in all of her activities, I have time to follow my personal interests."

He reached out his hand, and she placed hers in it. "Thanks for leveling with me. I'm happy I was around when you decided to get a new life."

"Me, too." Believing it was time to take the focus off her before he asked questions she didn't want to answer, Aimee said, "How was your day?"

"Busy. It's hard sometimes to balance my counseling work with the Siblings commitments and other things I like to do. But I thank God I have a good practice, which supports me and also gives me the opportunity to be involved in humanitarian activities like Siblings and civic affairs. I'm really enjoying being associated with the bicentennial committee. I'm learning things about our city I never knew before. Besides, it's a break from the heavier stuff. We had a meeting at three o'clock today."

"Any new plans?"

"Not really, but we made some final decisions on matters we've been discussing for months. We're going to run several TV and newspaper ads encouraging residents to invite their families from other areas to the celebration, and we're asking local graduates from the various schools to send invitations to their alumni who no longer live in Benton. I agreed to help the committee keep track of previous alumni who respond."

"Did you make any more decisions about the memorial to the teacher you mentioned?"

Jacob waited while the waitress placed their entrées on the table before he answered.

"Oh, you mean David Harwood. Nothing new, but I will be presenting the plaque and giving a short eulogy after all. The plaque will placed permanently in the office of the board of education."

They chatted lightly during the leisurely meal, and Aimee felt more at ease now that they weren't discussing private things.

When they left the restaurant, a half moon shed its pale light around the area, and before Jacob opened the car door for her, he hugged her to him. A smile of enchantment touched his lips. "This is the most pleasant evening I've enjoyed for a long time. We'll have to come here again."

"Thanks. I'd love that."

A car pulled in beside them, breaking the tender moment. Jacob sighed, released Aimee and opened the car door. They arrived at the theater in time for the eight-thirty showing. It seemed natural to Aimee for them to hold hands as they watched the tragic story of a college that had lost the majority of its football team and coaches in a plane wreck. The efforts of the college administration and coaches to rebuild their football program, and the odds they overcame, were encouraging to her as she contemplated living her life without Samantha as the focal point.

When they returned to the car, Jacob moved across the seat until he was close enough to Aimee to put his arm around her. From the dim light in the parking lot, she could see his eyes shining down at her. Her pulse pounded, and her heart gave a panic-stricken lurch as he lowered his face to hers. Her eyes automatically closed as his nearness wrapped around her like a warm blanket.

But when his face came closer and she felt his soft gentle breath on her face, her eyes flew open of their own accord. She pushed him away.

"No, Jacob, we're rushing things. This is going way too fast for me." She moved away until her back was against the car door.

"I only wanted to *kiss* you," he said quietly, but he started the car and drove out of the parking lot.

She scanned his face, distressed by his tense expression. They traveled to her home in silence, and Aimee didn't know what to say or do. She hadn't meant to get so close so soon, or maybe she had. Should she apologize?

How could she tell him that she *wanted* him to kiss her, but the way she was reacting to his embrace scared her? Not that she was afraid of Jacob, but of her own emotions.

When Jacob parked in front of her house, they turned toward each other, and almost simultaneously, the words came from both of their lips, "I'm sorry…"

Aimee was silent as Jacob continued, "Sorry that I ruined our evening. We were having such a good time."

"I don't consider it ruined," Aimee said,

hoping she could ease the hurt in Jacob's eyes. "I need to come to terms with a few hang-ups in my emotional life before I get too close to anyone again." She laid her hand on his arm. "Believe me, it doesn't have anything to do with you personally. Thanks for the good dinner and the movie."

She hugged him briefly, then opened the car door and stepped out before he could turn off the engine. Knowing that he was watching her, Aimee tried to walk sedately, when what she wanted to do was bolt into the house, go to her bedroom and try to figure out what had happened to her. She unlocked the door and waved to Jacob as he drove away.

The house was quiet and Samantha was asleep with the night-light on in her room. Aimee undressed and went to bed, but she couldn't go to sleep. She kept wondering what it would have been like to be kissed by Jacob, and if she'd missed her only chance to find out.

Several times during the week when the phone rang, if Aimee answered, Samantha would hang around to see who was calling. Once on the way to school, when Aimee paused at a stoplight, she had asked, "Do you have another date with Mr. Mallory this week?"

Aimee had kept her eyes on the traffic and answered easily, "No," but she gave no explanation. Perhaps she should tell Samantha that she didn't have to worry about her mother seeing Jacob again, but Aimee wasn't ready to promise that.

Chapter Eight

Rejected again! The words rolled over and over in Jacob's mind as he drove home. He had hoped that he'd finally dealt with the pain he'd experienced when Megan Russell had been unfaithful to him, apparently loving another man more than she did him. Obviously, he hadn't. Now Aimee had rejected him, and that hurt seemed worse than what his parents and his fiancée had done to him.

Jacob hadn't told Gran that he was going out with Aimee, and as he ran the next morning, he decided not to tell her. She had given up encouraging him to marry, and he hadn't wanted her to get her hopes up again. Besides, he didn't know that he wanted to marry anyone, although he had started thinking about it after he met Aimee. He had thought that he could be happy with her, but she apparently wasn't interested in him as much as he was in her.

Thinking about the rift between himself and Aimee led him to think about his father once again. He knew nothing of his paternal family. If he were ever to seriously consider marriage, he should learn something about his background. Although his short-lived relationship with Aimee may be over, that didn't mean he might not find someone else who interested him. After his run was finished, he went into the main house to see his grandmother, who was listening to the morning news on television. She turned off the TV, always ready to talk to her grandson.

"Sit down," she invited.

"Not now. I have an early appointment, and I need to leave in an hour, but I've been thinking about my father. I've never been interested in knowing anything about him, but I suppose I should find out about him for health reasons. Based on what you know about him, should I try to find him?"

"Yes. Your father was a personable young man—certainly no one for you to be ashamed of. I agree that you should know something about your ancestry, but I can't be much help. Your parents married secretly, and I didn't know about the marriage until you were on the way."

"Do you suppose it was a marriage of necessity

because Mom was pregnant?" he asked hesitantly, dreading the answer. "Maybe he was forced into the marriage and that's why he took off."

She shook her head. "I don't think so. Your mother kept a framed copy of the wedding certificate in her room, and they had been married almost a year when you were born. I saw your father once. He came home with Marybeth when my husband died. As far as I could tell, they were in love. He seemed like a nice guy to me, and I couldn't believe that he just walked off and left her."

"Mother wouldn't talk to me about him."

"I know," Gran said sympathetically. "Marybeth didn't mention his name after she came home. After her death, I packed away a box of things I thought you might want someday. They're yours whenever you're ready for them."

"At long last, I think I'm ready to deal with the past," Jacob said wryly. "I have to hurry now, but I'll get the box later and look through it." He leaned over and kissed his grandmother's cheek. "Thanks again for all you've done for me, Gran. It's hard to find the words to tell you how much I appreciate you."

She patted his cheek. "It's been a pleasure. You know that!"

That evening when he came home from work, before he went to his apartment, Jacob went into the main house. He found his grandmother in the kitchen. "I have a free evening," he said, "so I might as well take that box now."

"It's upstairs in Marybeth's room," Gran said, adding, "I got it out of the closet, but it's rather heavy, so I left it for you to carry down."

He perched on a high stool close to the sink where she was working. "You said you didn't know much about my father or his family, but tell me what you do know."

"He was taking premed studies," Grand answered, "but when Marybeth got pregnant, he quit school, to make a living for them. I'm reasonably sure that his parents were still living at that time, and that there were other children besides your father. I know nothing else. Perhaps I should have tried to locate him after Marybeth died."

"I still can't decide if it's a bad idea to start asking questions now," Jacob said slowly.

"I consider it a good idea," Gran assured him. "Even if there isn't much in the box, you can probably trace your relatives quickly on the Internet."

"But what if I find them and they aren't interested in me?" Jacob questioned, wondering if he might be opening up a communication that would lead to more rejection. "They would surely have known that they had a grandchild."

Gran paused, as if in thought, before she answered. "I don't know that you have to make contact with them if you don't want to. But, who knows, they may have tried to find you and couldn't."

The contents of the box were a disappointment to Jacob. In addition to the framed wedding certificate, there was a photograph of his parents on their wedding day. They looked very happy. There were a few baby pictures, which he assumed were of him. He looked through a manila folder of college papers, and when he had almost given up, he found an unfinished family tree, probably prepared for his father in his medical studies, which listed the names of his father's parents—Andrew and Elizabeth Mallory.

After Jacob spent several evenings searching for the names on his computer, he had a jumble of information about the Mallory family, with six Andrew Mallorys listed. Yet nothing he discovered linked him for sure to any of them.

Although he thought that this new interest might take his mind off of Aimee, it didn't. She was the last thing on his mind before he went to sleep and the first thing in his thoughts when he woke up. More than once he lifted the phone to call her, but he didn't. As Sunday approached, he started to wonder if Aimee would come to church.

Concentrating on finding his family roots kept him from constantly thinking about her. While he had been searching the Internet, he had come across a company that claimed they had a ninety-eight percent success rate in bringing together separated siblings and parents. He checked the references for the service and believed it would be reliable. Thinking that an organization like that could make a more efficient search than he personally could, especially considering the short amount of time and information he had, Jacob contacted a representative by e-mail and sent in the personal information requested. Now all he had to do was wait and see.

Without Jacob's frequent calls, the week dragged by for Aimee, and she couldn't decide if she should go to church on Sunday. She knew if she didn't go, she would make Erica suspicious, but if she did attend worship, as alert as Erica was, she would probably notice immediately the tension between Aimee and Jacob. In one way, she wanted to talk to somebody about her attraction for Jacob, and if she did, Erica would be the one, but she wasn't sure she could talk about it yet.

While she struggled with the problem, she received a call from Jacob's grandmother. "Aimee, this is Stella Milton. You know, Jacob's grandmother."

"Oh, yes, how are you, Mrs. Milton?"

"I have a nasty cold, and I'm staying in for a few days. I know you have an interest in our Siblings program, and I also remember that you're short of time until after school is out. But I think I have something you might like to do in the meantime."

Aimee hesitated briefly. "I'll help if I can. What do you have in mind?"

"We've been directed to a young girl who's living with an elderly grandmother. The one who recommended her to Siblings said that the grandmother provides the necessities, but the girl doesn't have anyone to *do* things with her. She could benefit from a woman's influence. Jacob told me that you have a teenage daughter, and I thought of you immediately as someone who would have the experience to meet the girl's needs. Your daughter might even want to befriend her, too."

Aimee rolled her eyes. Apparently, Jacob hadn't told his grandmother much about Samantha. To befriend an underprivileged girl would be the last thing her daughter would do. Aimee hesitated. To take this assignment would cause friction with Samantha again. Without Jacob's calls, they'd been getting along amiably for several days now, and she hated to rock the boat. But Aimee felt that she should make the commitment.

"I'll try it," she said slowly.

"Good," Stella said. She sneezed and excused herself. "If you're going to be out today, you might stop by the office and pick up the papers we have on her. Jacob will be working there this morning. Or I can ask him to bring them to church tomorrow."

Aimee's errands for the day would take her to that vicinity and that would give her a good excuse to see Jacob without seeming to pursue him. Perhaps this would provide an opportunity for them to talk about what had happened on their date. Fleetingly, Aimee wondered if this was a ruse on Stella's part to bring Jacob and her together, that is, if Stella even knew they'd been seeing each other.

"I'll be shopping this morning in that area, and I'll stop by," Aimee agreed. "How long will Jacob be there?"

"Until midafternoon, I'm sure. He has a meeting of the bicentennial committee tonight," Stella added.

"I'll go sometime before noon. I'll look over the girl's application, and if I don't think I can handle the assignment, I'll let you know."

"I appreciate this," Stella said. "By the way, the girl's name is Chloe Spencer."

The name rang a bell in Aimee's memory, and she thought the girl might have been one of the students at her school.

The phone rang again as soon as Aimee hung up, and it was Jennifer calling for Samantha.

"Hi, Mrs. Blake. Is Sam up yet?"

"Yes, I think so. I'll check and see."

"Wait. Sam said she was sorta grounded," Jennifer said calmly, "so I'll ask you first. My mom and aunt are going to a big mall in Richmond this morning. Dad's gone, and she won't leave me by myself all day. I can ask two of my friends to hang out with me at the mall while they shop. Madison's going. Can Sam go, too?"

"I have no objection to that. Let me call Samantha."

When Aimee heard Samantha answer, she pushed the stop button on her phone. She had been wondering how to explain to Samantha that she was going to the Siblings office. With Samantha out of town all day, it would be a good time to see Jacob, because now that she had a reason, Aimee was eager to contact him.

When she finished talking with Jennifer, Samantha ran upstairs. "Mom, thanks for letting me go. Can I have an advance on next week's allowance?"

"No, but I'll donate twenty dollars to the day's outing. I hope you have fun."

"You're awesome. Thanks!"

It was ten o'clock when Jennifer's mother

stopped by for Samantha. Aimee walked out to the six-passenger van to thank Mrs. Nibert for the invitation.

After she waved them on their way, Aimee took a deep breath of the fresh air that blew from the mountain range to the west and walked back into the house with a whole day before her free from maternal responsibilities. For the first time since she'd become a mother, that pleased her. Didn't that prove she was maturing as much as Samantha?

She was thankful that Stella had given her a reason to see Jacob without appearing to be pursuing him but should she call and tell him she was coming?

She decided against it. Perhaps his reaction to a surprise visit might provide a better indication of how he felt about her.

She drove over to Jacob's building and parked. After learning from the receptionist that he was in the Siblings office, she walked upstairs. The door was open, and he was working at the computer. When she walked in, he turned quickly in his chair, stood up and started toward her. Her pulse leaped with excitement, for he made no attempt to hide the fact that he was happy to see her. Regardless of the friction the last time they were together, obviously a web of attraction was building between them.

"Gran told me you were coming by today." He

motioned to a couch at one side of the room. "Sit down."

"She mentioned a girl I might work with, and I came by to look at her application," Aimee explained.

He picked up a file from the top of his desk, sat beside her on the couch and handed the folder to her. A photo was on the front of the file, and underneath was the information, *Chloe Spencer, fourteen years old.*

"Chloe Spencer," Aimee said slowly. "She seems familiar to me. Maybe she was a student at our school."

"She probably was. There's a brief description."

Aimee scanned the girl's profile. "I'm sure I remember her. Her mother died when she was in the fifth grade, and she came to live with her grandmother. That put her in our school district. I think she was in Aimee's class."

"Chloe's grandmother is concerned because she isn't making friends. She receives good care at home, but her grandmother thinks she needs the influence of an adult who's younger than she is. It was Gran's idea that you would be a good choice because you have a teenage daughter, who might get interested in Chloe, too."

Aimee gave him a straightforward glance. "You know that isn't going to happen."

"Probably not, but I didn't reveal any of your family problems to Gran."

"Thanks. What about Chloe's father?"

A momentary look of discomfort spread across Jacob's face when he said, "He apparently abandoned Chloe and her mother."

"Poor girl," Aimee said, and looked away because she knew Jacob was thinking of his own abandonment.

Aimee glanced through the folder, knowing that if she took Chloe under her wing, it was going to cause more challenges with Samantha. But she also considered what Samantha's life would have been like if she'd had no mother. "I don't know how much time I can give Chloe, but I'll try to help."

"I know it won't be easy for you to add something else to your schedule," Jacob said, "but I'll give you any support I can."

"Do I keep the file?" Aimee asked.

Jacob shook his head. "I need the original papers, but I'll give you copies of everything we have. If you're free this afternoon, I'll take you and introduce you to Chloe and her grandmother."

"I have the whole day," Aimee said. "Samantha went with friends to a mall in Richmond. It will be late before she gets home."

A buzzer sounded on Jacob's desk, and he stood and pushed the intercom button. "Mr. Mallory,

I'm leaving now," the receptionist said. "Is there anything I need to do before I go?"

"Not that I can think of," he said after a moment's hesitation. "Lock the door, please."

"Have a nice weekend," she said.

"You, too."

Then Jacob made several copies of Chloe's papers and returned to sit beside Aimee. "I've missed talking to you this week," he said.

Aimee felt her face flushing, and she looked away, unable to interpret the message in his eyes. "And I missed hearing from you. I wanted to call and apologize for ruining our evening, but I stopped short of picking up the phone."

"You had every right to shove me away," he said sincerely. "I was taking a lot for granted."

Tears formed in her eyes. "You shouldn't take the blame. To be honest, I wanted you to kiss me, but I have some mixed feelings from the past that I apparently haven't resolved."

Bitterness came into his expression, and he said, "I have a few of those, too, but let's talk about them over a sandwich. We have a lunch-room downstairs, and Gran keeps it supplied with snack foods. Or, if you'd prefer, we can stop and eat on our way to Chloe's house."

"Eating here will be fine."

He put Chloe's file back in the cabinet and

locked the office door behind them. The lunchroom was small, but big enough for two tables, with seating space for eight people. A refrigerator and a microwave were available, and a coffeemaker stood on the counter. Aimee saw Gran's influence in the bright pink ruffled curtains and the dainty white tablecloths. A small sink and dishwasher were centered under the picture window.

"A cheerful room," Aimee said.

"We have clients and visitors in here occasionally, and they seem to appreciate the homelike atmosphere," Jacob told her as he checked out the food available.

"Do you counsel adults, too?" Aimee queried.

"Yes, that's my main business and how I make my living, but my heart is with the Siblings program." He opened the refrigerator door. With a grin, he said, "We don't have an extensive menu. There are individual pizzas, cold cuts and cheese cubes, bread and crackers. Also, apples and grapes." He opened a cabinet over the refrigerator and set out a deli bag. "Cookies for dessert."

"Sounds like a feast," Aimee said. "I'll have an apple, cheese cubes and crackers."

"I'll have the same," he said as if he was talking to a waitress. "Fix yourself a beverage. There are bottles of pop in the refrigerator. I'll wash the apples."

"What would you like to drink?" Aimee asked.

"A glass of root beer."

Jacob set a two-liter bottle of root beer out, and Aimee filled glasses for both of them and added ice. She took the cheese cubes and crackers and put them on the table, then sat down. When he joined her with two apples cut into sections, Jacob reached his hand across the table.

"Let's thank God for the food." His prayer was brief, but the closing sentence touched Aimee's heart. "God, I thank You for giving Aimee and me the opportunity to help this teenager. Guide us as we work together in Your will. Amen."

Before he started eating, he said, "I'll call Chloe's grandmother and see if it's all right for us to stop by this afternoon. That way we'll know how much time we have for lunch."

After he spoke with Chloe's grandmother, he covered the mouthpiece and asked, "She can see us at two-thirty. Is that too late for you?"

"No."

After he hung up, Aimee said, "It will be quite late when Samantha gets back. In case you've wondered about how we're dealing with her rebellion, we're a bit wary of each other, but there isn't any open hostility."

"I'm sure you'll make the right decisions," he

assured her. Uncertainty crept into his expression as he continued, "Kids go through tons of problems today that we didn't have to deal with, although I experienced plenty of traumatic situations. As a matter of fact, one of the reasons I went into counseling was because I'm still affected by some of the childhood situations that disillusioned me. When I considered a profession, I knew I wanted to help others overcome the kinds of problems that had marked my youth."

"It surprises me that you have these frustrations," Aimee said. "You come across as a guy who has it all together."

"Perhaps I do in many ways," he said, "but I'll admit to you that my past has kept me from forming any serious relationships."

Aimee lowered her eyes rather than meet his, which seemed clouded with visions from the past.

"Are you interested enough to listen?" Jacob asked. "If you consider me only a casual acquaintance and are ready to stop seeing me, you may not want to hear what I have to say."

Experiencing conflicting emotions, Aimee hesitated. "Although I don't know where it will lead, I *do* want to see more of you. Truthfully, Jacob, I've been alone so long I'm afraid to change my life. But I believe God will guide us, and whatever comes of our time together, we can accept it, for we'll know that it's His plan for us. Right now, I'm happy to have you for a friend."

He nodded understandingly. "I've told you how my father deserted me and that Mother didn't have much time for me."

"Yes, I remember."

"I found a picture of him in some of her things, and I seem to favor him. Perhaps every time she saw me, she wished she had him instead of me. But I've been sensitive about rejection ever since then."

Somewhat puzzled, Aimee said, "But that happened so long ago."

"There's more." Jacob stood and wandered aimlessly around the small room for several minutes. When he spoke, his voice was totally emotionless and the atmosphere of the room seemed frigid. "Shortly before I graduated from high school, I became engaged to a girl I'd been dating for two years. She betrayed me, then rejected me for another man. So when you shoved me away last week, it was as if you were rejecting me, too."

"But—" she started to protest, and he interrupted, "I know, I know. It was childish to react the way I did. But because your pushing me away hurt so much, it seems to indicate that you're more important to me than any other woman has been. Does any of this make sense to you?"

Her eyes were misty. "Yes, and I'm flattered. I

don't suppose I should ask, but is your former fiancée still living in Benton?"

"No. I haven't heard from her since I went away to college. I don't know where she is. I'm not carrying a torch for her, if that's what you think. It was the original hurt that still gnaws at my spirit occasionally."

Sounding more cheerful than she felt, Aimee said brightly, "Then let's just forget the things that have happened between us so far and start over again."

"I don't want to forget some of them," he said, smiling slightly. "We've had a good time together, and it seems to give me a new lease on life just to visit with you on the phone."

"Then let's learn from our mistakes and move on. How about that?" Aimee asked cheerfully.

He reached for her hand and kissed her fingers. "That's what I hoped you would say, because that's what I want to do."

He pushed back from the table, gathered her into his arms and held her snugly. For a long moment she felt as if she were floating on a cloud, but with a sigh, Jacob released her.

"Perhaps we'd better go," he said regretfully.

At that moment, Aimee would have been satisfied just to stay within the circle of his arms. Still, she'd said they were going to be friends. She'd set the terms; now she'd have to live with them.

Chapter Nine

The Spencer home was located in an older section of Benton, but Aimee was pleased to note that the one-story house was painted and in good repair in contrast to some of the other houses in the neighborhood.

The door was opened by a brown-haired girl.

"Chloe?" Jacob said. She nodded.

"I'm Jacob Mallory from Substitute Siblings." He touched Aimee's shoulder. "This is Aimee Blake."

With a slight smile, the girl said softly, "I know Mrs. Blake. Come in."

"I recognize you, too, Chloe," Aimee said as they entered the house. "I thought your name sounded familiar. You must have been a student at Eastside Elementary."

Chloe nodded her head. "Yes. I moved to

Benton when I was in the fifth grade. Grandma is in the living room."

Chloe was a smaller girl than Samantha, with delicately carved facial features. Green eyes beamed from the pale gold undertones of her face. Her straight auburn hair flowed gently around her shoulders, resulting in a rare beauty.

They followed Chloe into a room to the right of the front door. A woman, probably in her late sixties, stood and shook hands with them. Her straight, gray hair was neatly shaped around her wrinkled cheeks, and she had the gentlest brown eyes Aimee had ever seen. A walker stood beside her chair.

"Please sit down. I'm Allie Slater."

Aimee and Jacob sat on the couch.

"It's good of you, Mrs. Blake, to take time for Chloe," Mrs. Slater said. "I know you're busy at school. And Chloe says you have a daughter, too."

"Yes, Samantha. She's fourteen, too."

"It worries me that Chloe doesn't make friends at school, and I'm not able to take her many places except to church. I thought Siblings would be helpful for her."

"This is my first assignment for Siblings," Aimee admitted, "but I'm sure that Chloe and I will get along all right." She turned to Chloe. "What are your favorite school subjects?"

A flush spread across Chloe's face. "I like music best."

"Oh, then you're singing in the spring chorale," Aimee assumed.

Shaking her head, Chloe answered, "No, I didn't try out for it."

"Why not?" Aimee persisted.

"I didn't think I'd be chosen, and that would have made me feel bad."

Aimee glanced toward Mrs. Slater, who shrugged her shoulders. "Chloe has always been a timid child. She sings in the youth choir at church, and she has a beautiful voice. I encouraged her to try out for the chorale."

"How long do you have to decide?" Aimee asked.

"They've started practicing already, but we sing some of the songs in music class," Chloe said.

"So maybe it's not too late for you to join," Aimee suggested. "Think about it. Now, for our day out, let's decide when and where. Actually, it will have to be a half day out, but would this coming Saturday afternoon suit you? We could take in a movie and have a snack afterward." Aimee looked toward Mrs. Slater. "Will that be okay with you?"

"If it's all right with Chloe." She looked at her granddaughter.

"Yes, ma'am, I'd like that."

"It's settled then." Aimee took a pen and notebook from her purse. "I'll give you my phone number if you need to postpone for any reason, but I'll call you before Saturday." They visited for a while, and Chloe showed Aimee her room.

An hour later, Jacob thanked Mrs. Slater and explained that they needed to go. "I have a meeting tonight," he told her. "It's nice to meet both you and Chloe."

"Excuse me for not going to the door with you, but my arthritis is acting up today, and when that happens, I can't get far away from my walker. Thanks so much for taking an interest in my granddaughter."

Chloe went with them to the door and stepped out on the porch. "Grandma is right," she said quietly, "I *am* too bashful to try out for the chorale, but the real reason is that I'd have to buy a black skirt and a white, long-sleeved blouse to be in it. Grandma can't afford it. She does the best she can, and I don't want to put her out."

"That's good of you, Chloe," Aimee said, and her heart was touched by the selflessness the girl exhibited. Unlike Samantha, who had grown up only thinking of herself. Aimee knew it was her fault as much as Samantha's that her daughter never hesitated to ask for anything she wanted.

Aimee put her arm around Chloe. "You go

ahead and try out for the chorale—if you are chosen, I'll see that you have the proper clothes."

"Oh, Mrs. Blake, I couldn't do that. But thank you."

"We can consider that part of my responsibility in being a Sibling for you. I'm sure we'll find something that isn't too expensive."

Chloe shook her head, but not very convincingly. Aimee gave her a quick hug.

Jacob's eyes were approving when he opened the car door. "That was good of you. Apparently, Mrs. Slater provides all of the necessities, but there isn't enough left for extras. But being a Sibling doesn't mean that you have to spend a lot of money."

"I'm a good shopper, so I'll be able to buy something suitable without spending tons of money. I have a feeling I'm going to benefit from this relationship as much as Chloe."

He drove back to the office and stopped beside Aimee's car. "When can I see you again?"

"I don't know. But let's keep in touch by phone. Although I don't have to go everywhere Samantha goes anymore, I am first of all a mother. I need to sort out my relationship with her. Everything else has to take second place."

Aimee made that statement, but her heart wasn't in it. Every time Jacob looked at her, she sensed the affection he wanted to give her. She longed for the protective comfort of his arms around her, and her instinctive response to his touch convinced her that she was indeed becoming fond of Jacob Mallory. Too fond? she wondered.

Jacob watched as she got into her car and drove away, wondering if any man who became a part of Aimee's life would have to accept second place to Samantha. Did he want that? He'd been hurt enough.

An invisible connection was building between them, as well as a physical awareness of each other. He sensed that Aimee was attempting to put a barrier between them by talking of her responsibility to Samantha. He couldn't believe that the attraction he felt for Aimee was one-sided. In his heart he believed that there was a tangible bond between them that even Samantha's hold on Aimee could not prevent from growing.

Samantha was bubbling with excitement when she got home about eight o'clock.

"Oh, Mom, we had a totally amazing day! Jennifer's mother is so fun to be with." She dug into the large plastic bag she carried. "Look at what I bought! I spent almost all of my money on this rope tote made out of recycled sails."

The bag didn't look like much to Aimee, but she

reminded herself that she wasn't fourteen. It was made of canvas, had ropes for handles and a large, blue five-pointed star sewn on one side with a red star on the other.

"Mrs. Toney, Madison's mom, said these bags go for almost one hundred fifty dollars in big-city department stores, but I bought this at a discount place."

Aimee didn't want to dim Samantha's joy, so she said, "It sure is a nice bag, and just the thing for you to take to Florida with you this summer."

Samantha draped the bag over her shoulder and pranced around the room. "That's the reason I bought it. Say, Mom, why don't you go to Florida with me this summer? Grammy told me to invite you to come along."

"That was nice of her, but I probably won't. Your father's family deserves to have some quality time alone with you. Thanks, anyway."

Aimee didn't like to suspect her daughter of ulterior motives, but after Samantha turned ten, she hadn't wanted her mother to go with her on the yearly visit. Aimee had always spent those two weeks housecleaning so she wouldn't miss Samantha so much. Why had her daughter changed? Didn't she want Aimee to be alone in Benton now that she had met Jacob?

"What'd you do today, Mom?"

Suspecting that Samantha wouldn't be happy about what she had done, Aimee silently prayed for guidance before she answered.

"Mrs. Milton, Jacob's grandmother, called this morning, mentioning that the Siblings organization had a teenager who needed a friend. Jacob and I had lunch together and then went to visit the girl."

Some the joy faded from Samantha's face, and Aimee was sorry to ruin her day.

"Mom, that is not fair! You're too busy now. I wish we'd never heard of Jacob Mallory. You're not the same since you've been seeing him."

Aimee couldn't dispute that, so she continued, "I've made plans to take her to a movie next Saturday afternoon."

"Well, what about me?"

"You're welcome to go with us. In fact, I want you to go."

Samantha ignored the invitation. "It's been months since you've taken me to a movie."

"And why haven't I?" Aimee asked with a lifting of her eyebrows.

Samantha blushed. For the past six months, when Aimee had mentioned going to a movie together, Samantha always said she wanted to see it with her friends.

"Who is this girl?" Samantha demanded, a petulant look on her lips.

"Chloe Spencer."

"What? I remember her. She's completely impossible. You start taking her places, and she'll ruin my life."

"I doubt that. She didn't impress me as the kind of girl who would go where she isn't wanted. Besides, this is between Chloe and me. You don't need to be involved unless you choose to."

"What are you going to do tomorrow?"

"We have church in the morning, and we can spend the afternoon together doing whatever you want to do."

A stubborn expression on her face, Samantha shook her head and turned toward the stairs. "No, thanks. Jennifer is coming over tomorrow afternoon, and she's going to help me study for my math test."

Jacob checked his e-mail when he got home from lunch and was pleased to see a message from the organization he'd contacted to search for his paternal relatives.

Dear Sir:

We have located a couple who are possibly your grandparents. All of the data checks out, and this was quite easy for us since these people are also searching for their grandson. We assume that you want to make the initial contact. Please forward the required fee, and we will give you the address and telephone number.

Jacob's first impulse was to erase the message and forget about it. But a strange longing came over him. He felt so rootless, and if these people were his father's parents, he would like to talk to them. It gave him a warm feeling to know that they wanted to meet him, too.

Jacob wrote a message to the man, sent the required fee, and within an hour had the names, mailing address, e-mail address and telephone number of the people who might be his grandparents. Would poking into the past cause him more anguish than he already felt?

He wanted to talk to someone about the situation, but he didn't want Gran worrying until he knew something more definite.

He dialed Aimee's number, and she answered on the first ring. "Is everything all right at your house?" he asked.

"Presumably," she said with a slight laugh. "Samantha and Jennifer are downstairs, supposed to be studying. Things are quiet down there, so I don't know if they're studying. But I'll hope for the best."

"It's a nice day. Could we drive down to Pioneer Park and hike for a while?"

"Yes, let's," Aimee said. "I haven't been to the park for a long time. I always enjoy the river walk."

"Good. I'll pick you up in an hour," Jacob said, and there was a trace of excitement in his voice.

"I'll be ready," Aimee told him.

Not until after she'd hung up did Aimee realize that she hadn't once considered Samantha in her decision. Slowly, she was learning to consider her own wants and needs.

Aimee checked the temperature, which was in the mid-sixties with the sun shining. Most of the river walkway was on level ground, but occasionally it wound uphill and through the forest. She put on a pair of jeans and a white sweatshirt, then she pulled on a pair of hiking shoes and heavy socks.

When she was ready, she went downstairs. She knocked on the door, and when Samantha or Jennifer didn't answer, she went in. The girls were sitting on Samantha's bed with headsets on, their eyes closed, apparently deeply engrossed in the music. *So much for studying!*

To get their attention, Aimee flipped the lights off and on a couple of times. The girls' eyes opened and they turned off the CDs.

"Hey, Mom! Where're you going?" Samantha asked with a smile.

"Jacob is picking me up. We're going to

Pioneer Park for a hike. I don't know how long we'll be gone."

"How cool is that?" Jennifer asked with her customary enthusiasm.

A sudden look of withdrawal erased Samantha's smile.

"Have fun," she said, turned up the music volume and closed her eyes. Jennifer looked at her friend, lifted her eyebrows in surprise, and gave Aimee a thumbs-up.

Shrugging her shoulders, Aimee closed the door and walked upstairs. She refused to let Samantha's attitude ruin her afternoon with Jacob. She watched from the foyer, and when he turned into her driveway, she went outside rather than wait for him to come to the house.

He got out and opened the door for her, then walked back around to the driver's side. They looked at each other, and Aimee sensed that Jacob was as excited about their outing as she was.

Both of them burst out laughing, and there was still a trace of laughter in her voice when Aimee said, "I don't know why I'm laughing, or why I'm so surprised at your appearance, but I just realized that this is the first time I've seen you dressed in casual clothes."

Jacob wore a flannel shirt and cutoff denim shorts, and he wore a ball cap.

"I guess it wouldn't be very convenient to hike in a business suit," she said, and they laughed again. Aimee had never felt so carefree in her life.

"You surprised me, too." He put the car in gear and backed into the street. "Maybe today we'll get behind the facade we present to the world and find our real selves."

Fastening her seat belt, Aimee said, "I hope so."

The drive to the park took less than thirty minutes, and when they got there, several cars were in the parking area near the head of the river trail. The municipal park had been established before Aimee was born, and activities here had always been a part of her life.

Jacob put a bottle of water and a first-aid kit in a backpack and slung it over his left shoulder before they walked toward the river and the trail opening. At the entrance, the trail was wide enough for them to walk side by side.

"Gran started bringing me to this park when I was just a kid. I'd play on the swings and slides, and we had picnics here, too. The church rented the big shelter every summer for our annual picnic."

"I was here often as a child, and I used to bring Samantha when she was growing up. Isn't it strange," Aimee said as they walked with the river in view, "that we might have been here at the same time and didn't meet each other? Wonder what would have happened if we'd met a long time ago."

Jacob shook his head. "It wasn't in God's plan for us to meet before, I suppose. Who knows? We might not have liked each other when we were younger."

When the trail narrowed, Aimee took the lead, and they didn't talk much until they reached a switchback that took them away from the river and into a large stand of oak and maple trees.

"We weave in and out of this forest for a mile or so, don't we?" she called over her shoulder to Jacob.

"Yes. There are benches along the way if you want to sit and rest."

When they reached a grove of pine trees, they were out of sight of the river now, and when Aimee approached the next wooden bench, she paused. "Let's stop here."

"Good." They'd been walking rather fast and Aimee breathed heavily as she sat down.

"Whew! I'm obviously out of shape," she said. "I need to start going to the Y."

"You've been setting a rapid pace. This is the halfway mark, and we can slow down now," Jacob said. "Most of the return trail is downhill."

"As I remember, this used to be a thicket of small pine trees. Now they're towering over us." She stretched out her legs.

"I'm ready to rest, too," Jacob said. "Besides,

I've got something to tell you. I think I may have found my father's family."

"You have? Are you happy or…?" Aimee's eyes complete the question.

"I don't know." He explained about the information he'd received. "I wanted to talk to you about it before I did anything further. I have the telephone number, but I can't decide whether to go through with this."

"Why?"

"I'm a coward," he said, laughing.

"You are not! You might have cold feet, but you're not a coward," Aimee said, a smile on her face.

"I don't want to talk to Gran about it until I call, that is, *if* I do."

"Of course you'll call," she encouraged him. "You've gone this far, you'll never be satisfied until you do."

"You're right. It means a lot to me to have your opinion. One reason I suggested taking this hike is that even though we've been together quite a lot, we still don't *know* each other."

"I don't understand."

"I don't know much about you before we met a few weeks ago, and I'd like to know more. Do you have any siblings, for instance?"

"I have two brothers, Brice and Kevin. They're both married and, between them, they've provided me with four nieces and three nephews. Brice lives in California, and Kevin and his family are in Louisiana. They come home every summer, and at the same time, so we have a big family reunion."

"Do you visit them?"

"No, but Mother and Daddy go to visit them, usually during the wintertime. The Christmases I've spent in Florida with Steve's family, my parents have gone to visit one of the boys." She chuckled at a happy memory. "Brice and I were only a year apart in age, and we fought most of the time when we were kids. In fact, my husband, Steve, and Brice were best friends. Brice was furious when Steve and I started dating, and he couldn't go everywhere we did."

"Lots of happy memories, huh?"

"I do have some good memories." She laid her hand on Jacob's arm. "Thanks for inviting me to come with you. I get so involved in the problems of the present, and when I do think about the past, I tend to remember incidents that I regret. You've helped me remember some of the good things today."

He took her hand and held it while they looked out through the pine forest where birds flew back and forth building their spring nests. Aimee was conscious of the change of life in the blossoming trees, the resurrection of the earth, and, even as she stretched out her hand for Jacob to hold, her thoughts turned to God and His place in their lives.

When they started on the trail again, Jacob said, "Have you had any thoughts about what we can do for entertainment on Fun in the Sun Day?"

"Yes, I have, and you may think it's a crazy thing to do," Aimee admitted with an embarrassed laugh. "I'm not very athletic, and I wondered if we could dress up as clowns, rent a loudspeaker system and play music. Every time the music stops, we can give prizes away."

"I like it," Jacob said quickly. "We can have everyone drop their names in a box, and we'd draw out several names at a time. I'll rent the sound system as well as a small tent. Any ideas about prizes?"

"We can have simple things like candy, fruit, even some inexpensive toys and trinkets. I'll contribute a hundred dollars for the gifts."

"I'll match it with another hundred, so we can be sure everyone gets something. It will be fun buying them. When can we go shopping?"

"We still have a month," Aimee calculated. "We can figure that out later."

"I'm not a good shopper," he warned.

"Ah, but I am," she commented with a carefree laugh. "All you have to do is carry the packages."

She threw her arm around his shoulders, and the

contact was electrifying. She moved away from him immediately, unwilling to meet his eyes or consider the jolt that innocent touch sent through her whole being.

They stopped in midstride, and Jacob pulled her into his arms. She felt his heart hammering, and she enjoyed his closeness for a few moments before she stepped away. Still wanting to touch him, she took his hand and they walked silently back to the car.

It was late afternoon by the time they returned to Benton. When they stopped at Aimee's house, she invited him to come in, but he said, "I'm going home to make that call before I lose what nerve I do have."

"Give me a call back," she said. "I'll be praying for you."

"That will help," he assured her.

Jacob's heart danced with excitement as he drove away from Aimee's house, and he knew he could handle whatever lay in wait for him on the other end of the phone.

As soon as he got home, Jacob went immediately to the phone. His hands trembled as he punched in the digits. On the third ring, a deep voice answered.

Jacob swallowed with difficulty and found he couldn't speak.

"Hello?" the man said again, questioningly.

Jacob's voice broken when he finally forced out the words, "I'm calling for Andrew Mallory."

"Speaking. Judging from my caller ID, is this Jacob Mallory?"

"Yes, sir," Jacob said, pleased that the introduction had been so easy. Still he hesitated, uncertain about what to say next.

"Why have you called, Jacob?" the man asked, not unkindly.

Half in anticipation, half in dread, Jacob took a deep breath. "A few weeks ago I decided to search for my father, Philip Mallory, who left my mother and me before I was a year old. My search led me to you, and I learned that you were looking for a grandson. The information I have says that you may be my grandfather."

"How old are you, Jacob?"

"Thirty-four."

"And where do you live?" the man persisted.

"Benton, Virginia," Jacob answered, then he posed a question of his own. "May I ask why you're searching for your grandson?"

Andrew Mallory started to speak, but his voice wavered, and Jacob sensed that the man was crying. After a few moments, Andrew sighed heavily, and his voice was filled with wretchedness when he finally spoke.

"I'm sorry, Jacob, but it's something I can't explain over the phone. Let's try to determine if there is a connection between us before we go any further. Will you send a picture of yourself, Jacob?"

"Yes, sir. I have a fairly recent photo, which I'll scan and e-mail to you."

Andrew seemed to have regained his composure, for his voice was steadier as he continued, "Jacob, I'm reasonably sure that you could be our grandson, at least to the extent that we want to meet you and personally discuss a possible relationship."

"I would like that, sir."

"We have a winter home in Florida," Andrew continued, "and that's where we are now. But our main home is in Malone, New York. My wife and I will be traveling northward along I-95 in June. If it's convenient, we'd like to stop and see you. How would we reach Benton from I-95?"

"Travel west on US-460. Benton isn't far from Lynchburg."

"We have GPS in our car, so as long as I have your address in Benton, I can find you. We will be delighted to find out if you are our grandson."

"I'd like to meet you, too," Jacob assured him.

"I can probably tell when I receive your picture if you are related to us," Andrew said, "but perhaps you look like your mother's family."

"I don't think so. My mother died when I was young, but I don't bear much resemblance to her."

"I'll look forward to receiving your picture. If you are our grandson, then we have many things to discuss, but I'd prefer to do that when we see you."

Jacob's throat tightened with emotion, and he spoke hesitantly. "But isn't there *anything* you can you tell me about my father now?"

There was no immediate answer, and Jacob was sorry he had asked.

In a hoarse whisper, Andrew Mallory said, "He is dead," and severed the phone connection.

Jacob held the phone away from his ear, shocked at what he had heard and also the dismal tone of the man's voice. He considered calling back and demanding more information, for how could he wait weeks to find out about his father?

He wondered again about his father's life. Had the desertion of his wife been the first step in a downward spiral that led to a tragic end? If this were so, maybe it would be better not to know. With mixed emotions, Jacob left his apartment and entered the main house to share his news with Gran.

Some grandmothers who had devoted so many years caring for their grandson might have resented the fact that Jacob's paternal family wanted to be part of his life now. But not Gran.

Hearing Jacob's news, tears of happiness sparkled in her eyes, and she put her arms around him. "I'm so happy for you. Did he sound pleased to talk with you?"

"Yes, until I asked him point-blank about my father, and—" Jacob's voice faltered "—he said he was dead."

"Oh," Stella said. "No details?"

"No, he hung up abruptly. I was tempted to call back and demand an answer," Jacob said, "but I couldn't do it. I sure hate to wait another six weeks to find out."

"The time will pass quickly," she said. "You'll be busy with plans for Fun in the Sun, as well as the bicentennial celebration."

"It will always be in my mind, but I can't do anything about it. If Andrew Mallory doesn't want to talk, I can't make him."

Jacob returned to his apartment and called Aimee.

"You made the phone call?" she asked right away.

"Yes, and talked to my grandfather, or at least," he amended, "the man who believes that he's my grandfather. He and my grandmother spend winters in Florida and go home to New York in a few weeks. He plans to stop and see me."

"Are you excited about it?"

"Not yet, but I probably will be by the time they get here." In a different tone, he added, "He said my father is dead, but wouldn't give me any details. I don't know what to think."

"Think positive. That's what you've been trying to teach me. Right?"

"I'm trying to, but six weeks is going to seem like a long time."

Chapter Ten

In spite of Samantha's displeasure, Aimee found herself looking forward to the afternoon with Chloe. Mrs. Slater came to the door with Chloe when Aimee stepped up on the porch.

Aimee noticed the absence of the walker and commented, "You're walking better today?"

"Much better. My arthritis comes and goes, and a lot of it is weather related. Maybe you don't hold with old-fashioned ideas about connections between the weather and ailments?"

Laughing, Aimee commented, "Oh, yes, I do! I often have pains in my legs before a big storm."

Mrs. Slater stepped out on the porch. "No storms today," she said, breathing deeply of a hint of spring wafted by a balmy south wind. Chloe came to the door, and the eagerness in the girl's face touched Aimee's heart.

"All ready?" Aimee asked.

Chloe nodded happily.

"We'll be back in a few hours," Aimee assured Mrs. Slater. "Do you still have my cell number?"

"Yes, but I won't worry. I know she's in good hands. Enjoy yourselves."

As they drove away from the sidewalk, Chloe said, "Guess what?"

A smile crossed Aimee's face. "I'm not good at guessing games. You'd better tell me."

"I tried out to sing in the chorale. The music teacher likes my voice. I'm in!"

Aimee gave her a high five and Chloe's face flushed with pride.

"That's awesome!" Aimee said. "After we see the movie, we'll celebrate by shopping for a new outfit for you. Remind me, what do you need?"

"A white blouse and long black skirt," Chloe said as she buckled her seat belt. "We need black shoes, too, but I have almost new ones."

After the movie, Aimee took Chloe to the same department store where she bought her own clothes. Aimee sensed that Chloe was sensitive about being unable to afford the items herself, and she was pleased when they found the blouse and skirt on sale. The total amount was low enough that Chloe accepted the gifts with very little protest.

During the afternoon Chloe asked a few timid questions about Samantha. She remembered her from Eastside and saw her sometimes at the high school, leaving Aimee with the impression that her daughter was somewhat of a role model for Chloe. She only hoped that she could continue helping Chloe without alienating Samantha.

Although Aimee had asked Samantha to go with them, she had refused, and when she returned home, Samantha didn't ask any questions about what they had done, which caused Aimee to wonder again if she should have taken the assignment. But when Jacob called wanting to know how she and Chloe had gotten along, his approval convinced Aimee that she was doing the right thing.

"She was really excited that she'd been chosen for the choral presentation," Aimee said happily, "and we found a nice outfit for her. Mrs. Slater was put off about the new clothes at first until I explained that it was one of the things I could do according to the Siblings regulations. She voiced her appreciation and let it go at that. I felt such a sense of accomplishment when I came home."

"Working with Siblings is a two-way street," Jacob assured her. "The more we give, the more we receive. It's kept me positive when I might otherwise have been negative about life in general."

Aimee was just hanging up with Jacob when

Erica called from the family room, "Hey! Anybody home?"

"I'm in the bedroom," Aimee answered. "Be there in a sec."

When Aimee joined her neighbor, Erica gave her an envelope. "Our registrations for the conference were accepted. I thought there was a possibility they might not be since we were late registering."

"Good," Aimee said, taking a deep breath. "The last month has been like a roller-coaster ride, more turmoil than I've had for years. I'm looking forward to getting away for a weekend."

"You deserve a break," Erica said.

Aimee agreed. "For one thing, I'm dealing with the change in my relationship with Samantha a lot better because my spiritual walk is more vital than it's been for years. I read the Bible and pray every night before I go to bed, but I still feel that I need time away from my distractions. Does that make sense?"

"Sure it does. And this conference might be just what you need to grow even closer to the Lord," Erica assured her. "It will give us an opportunity to share our concerns with other women who are experiencing the same problems we are. And there are many opportunities for private meditation and prayer, too."

* * *

The next three weeks before the conference passed so quickly that more than once Aimee almost wished she hadn't agreed to go.

She made a point to see Chloe or make contact with her every week. She took Samantha to a regional cheerleading competition. They went shopping for new clothes. And they talked. Samantha even said she was sorry for the night she had interrupted Aimee and Jacob, although she said she still didn't think Aimee had any business dating him. Well, at least they were talking. As Aimee juggled her time, it seemed that there wasn't much left for Jacob anyway. When she considered how much she missed seeing him, she knew that Jacob was a factor to be considered in her future, and Samantha was just going to have to get used to it.

So when Jacob called and asked if they could get together and go shopping for the Fun in the Sun prizes, she agreed. The opportunity to be alone with him for a few hours sent her spirits soaring. She knew the day was fast approaching when she would have to deal seriously with her reaction to his presence, and let him know that he was more than just a friend.

Jacob picked her up just after noon on the Saturday before the Fun in the Sun event, and they drove to a mall on the outskirts of Benton. They found a variety store that was going out of business and all of their stock was half-price. They were able to buy more with their two hundred dollars than they expected.

Jacob made several trips to his van with their purchases, and after they spent all the money they'd budgeted, he said, "We have enough items to give every kid and even their parents several prizes."

"That gives me a great feeling," Aimee said. With a grin, she added, "Perhaps it's the company, but I don't know when I've enjoyed a day more."

Jacob didn't even consider that they were standing in a popular shopping center when he suddenly tipped her chin up and kissed her. Aimee didn't pull back this time. She returned his kiss without hesitation, then gently pulled away, lifting her hand and caressing his cheek and jaw before stepping out of the circle of his arms.

Jacob watched as she turned from him and sat down in the van. Friends, ha! How much longer could they fool themselves into believing that the emotions they were experiencing evolved from a casual friendship?

When they arrived at Aimee's home, Jacob turned off the engine, but when Aimee invited him inside, he said, "No, I won't stay. But while you were shopping, I bought something for you."

He reached under the car seat and handed her a sack. She eyed him with curiosity, thinking he'd probably bought a gag gift for her like the ones they'd bought for the children. She glanced quickly at him, surprised to find that he'd bought her a bottle of expensive perfume in the lavender scent she always wore.

"Well, thank you," Aimee stammered. "But why?"

He seemed a little embarrassed, but he said, "One of the things I noticed about you the first day we met was the fragrance of lavender that surrounded you. When I saw the perfume on the shelf today, it reminded me of our first meeting at school, and I wanted to buy it. Our time together has been special to me, Aimee."

Not caring whether Samantha would see, Aimee leaned toward Jacob and kissed his cheek. "That's about the nicest thing anyone has ever said to me. I've enjoyed getting to know you, Jacob, for *you* are special to me."

The Saturday Fun in the Sun event was a hit, and at the end of the day, Gran assured Aimee and Jacob that their appearance as clowns had been the highlight of the day. Their booth *had* been popular, and as Aimee gave away dozens of gifts to the kids, she tried unsuccessfully to put Samantha's opinion of their work out of her mind.

Aimee modeled her clown suit for Samantha and invited her to go to Fun in the Sun Day. After one horrified glance at Aimee's costume, she said, "No, thanks. You think it's cool to be dressed up like that? I don't! I hope no one knows you're my mother."

But when Jacob took her home at the end of the day, he said, "You were super today. And although I don't know what caused that sad look in your eyes, try to forget it by thinking of the kids and their parents you made happy."

"Thanks," she said. "I don't regret a minute of the time and effort it took to accomplish what we did. I've had a wonderful day. I just wish Samantha would have joined us."

Aimee was thrilled that the changes in her life were making her less self-centered—and less Samantha-centered. But when was Samantha going to see that the world did not revolve around her?

The week before the women's retreat flew by with little time for Aimee to worry about her daughter. Samantha seemed less sullen, though, and her math grade was better. She didn't even seem to mind too much that Aimee was leaving for the weekend, although that could be because Samantha knew it would keep her away from Jacob.

Erica and Aimee took Friday off from work for final preparations and left midmorning for the three-hour drive to Camp Serenity. Aimee's parents intended to pick up Samantha and Madison after school and take them to the farm, so Aimee was free to relax and enjoy the retreat.

They drove Aimee's car but shared the driving on the hundred-mile trip into the mountainous region where the camp was located.

They were assigned to the third floor of a dormitory, and by the time she lugged all of her luggage up the two flights of stairs, Aimee wished she had packed fewer clothes. She hadn't been camping since she was a teenager, and she'd forgotten that the atmosphere was laid-back and that jeans and shirts were more practical than some of the dressier stuff she'd packed.

When they finally settled into an austere room with four bunk beds, a closet without a door and two folding chairs, Aimee looked out the window at the awesome view.

"Oh, my," she gasped. "If I don't see or hear anything else, that view is worth the trip. We lucked out on a room."

Although the windowpanes were flyspecked

and streaked, she could see the mountains, where blooming dogwood and redbud added a splash of white and fuchsia among the pine trees and cedars. In a meadow at the foot of the mountains, two deer grazed.

"The scenery *is* beautiful," Erica agreed. "Other times when I've been here, I skipped some of the sessions and wandered off alone. I had planned to take you on a nature hike before dinner, but I'm winded. Let's rest a while."

"I've wondered about our cabinmates. I hope we get along."

Erica climbed the few steps to an upper bunk and stretched out on her back. "Taking potluck with roommates can be iffy sometimes, but there's little risk at a church conference. I'm sure we'll have a good time."

Aimee continued to enjoy the scene before her for several minutes before she unpacked her suitcase and hung a few things in the closet. Noticing that there were only two hangers, and those were bent and rusty, she commented, "I see why you told me to bring my own hangers."

"Yeah. We won't have any luxuries, only a place to sleep and eat. But it's good for us to rough it for a few days. Have you tried your bunk?"

"No. Why?"

"This bed feels like a block of concrete." Erica

squirmed uncomfortably before adding, "But I can stand it for one weekend."

"I didn't expect to have top-notch accommodations but I figure I will miss my comfortable bed. Oh, that must be one of our roommates coming," Aimee said as footsteps sounded in the hallway.

A woman with dark, snappy eyes and a regal way of carrying herself entered the room. Her straight dark hair was shoulder length, and she appeared to be at least six feet tall.

"I'm your roomie," she said as she surveyed the space. "Lori Alexander."

Aimee moved toward her and took her outstretched hand. "Glad to meet you, Lori. I'm Aimee Blake, and this is my friend, Erica Snyder."

"We were wondering who our roommates would be," Erica said as she sat up in the bunk and waved to Lori.

"I'm it," Lori said as she put down her suitcase and draped her garment bag over the edge of the bunk. "There will be only the three of us. My sister planned to attend, but she had to cancel this morning. We live in Alexandria."

"We're from Benton," Aimee said.

Surprise spread across Lori's face. "Well, well, it *is* a small world. I lived in Benton until I was twenty. I graduated from Paramount High School.

In fact, I'm planning to come to Benton for the bicentennial."

"You and several thousand others," Erica said. "A lot of plans are being made."

"I've lived in Benton most of my life, but I graduated from East High, rather than Paramount," Aimee said, "so I didn't go to school with you."

"I didn't move to Benton until after I was out of high school," Erica said, "so I wasn't in school with either of you."

"We'll soon get acquainted. This is going to be a fun weekend," Lori exclaimed. "I haven't been back to my hometown since my family moved. You'll have to tell me what's happened in Benton since I left."

The sound of laughing, talking and merrymaking in general sounded throughout the building, and Erica groaned. "Besides having to climb the steps, there's a disadvantage to living on the top floor," she said. "All the noise comes up the stairs, and there will be about fifty women in this building—some of them talking and laughing all night. Don't expect to get much sleep."

Aimee glanced at her watch. "It's only forty-five minutes until dinner."

"That will give me time for a shower," Lori said. She put her suitcase on the floor at the foot of her bunk, opened it and took out a cosmetics case. "If I'm not finished by the time you want to go, don't wait for me. We'll meet up later." She headed down the hall to the shower room.

"Nice lady," Aimee commented.

"Yes, she is. This is the first time I've met her, but I've heard of her. She's a great vocalist. I'm pretty sure I saw her name on the program for special music."

After dinner, Aimee and Erica moved to the large auditorium, with seating for three hundred, but since the enrollment of the conference was considerably less than that, everyone was asked to sit near the platform in a compact group. The subject of Pam Baker, the featured speaker, was Focus on the Future—not the Past.

Aimee found it difficult to guess Pam's age, but she had a sprinkling of gray in her dark hair and Aimee judged that she was in her late forties. Of average height, she had high cheekbones, large hazel eyes in a tanned complexion and an uptilted nose, on which was perched a pair of reading glasses. She had a warm, friendly smile.

She was the author of several books on spiritual growth, and after her first presentation, an announcement was made that her books would be for sale throughout the conference. Pam would also be available for fifteen-minute counseling sessions with any conferee interested in speaking to her privately.

Although Aimee had never felt free to discuss her past marital difficulties with anyone, she sensed that she could talk to Pam without embarrassment. For one thing, she would probably never see the woman again, so she wouldn't mind sharing her inadequacies. She signed up for a conference, and long after Erica and Lori had gone to sleep, Aimee lay awake, wondering what effect Pam's words might have on her relationship with Jacob.

Aimee met Pam the next morning in a small room adjacent to the chapel. One wall was covered with a pastoral mural featuring a group of children playing in a field of flowers. There was no window in the room, and it seemed to Aimee that she and Pam were in a world of their own, free from outside distractions.

Seated opposite each other, with a small table between them, Pam said, "Let's pray first, Aimee."

Covering Aimee's folded hands with her own, Pam prayed, *"Our Father, this is my first meeting with Aimee, but I feel a bond between us already. Only You can meet her needs, but I pray that You will use me as an instrument to help her. In the precious name of Your Son, I pray. Amen."*

Pam released Aimee's hands. "Now, tell me about yourself."

"I've been a widow for almost fourteen years, and I have a fourteen-year-old daughter, Samantha."

Aimee's voice must have mellowed when she mentioned her daughter's name, for Pam smiled. "The love of your life!"

"Yes, very much so. My husband died suddenly of an aneurysm when Samantha was a baby, so it's just been the two of us," Aimee explained. "She doesn't remember her father."

"I'm a widow, too, so I can empathize with you. Go on."

Aimee quickly relayed her concern of the past few months when Samantha had become rebellious, more inclined to spend time with her friends and confide in them rather than her mother.

"That's to be expected," Pam said. "It's all a part of growing up. Both of my children have graduated from college and are on their own, but when my son was in his teens, we went head to head most of the time. By the grace of God, he's now a levelheaded young man, but I often wondered if that day would ever come. Tell me how you've handled this situation?"

Conscious that she only had fifteen minutes, Aimee quickly admitted that she'd spoiled her daughter, then explained the tough love she'd been trying now as a means to train Samantha for adulthood.

Pam nodded approvingly as Aimee talked. "Which brings me to another question—how is your spiritual life?"

"Improving now, but I've been a wayward Christian for several years. While trying to juggle my job and taking care of Samantha, I stopped going to church. I regret that."

"We can never change the past, only look to the future. It seems to me that you're on the right course with your daughter. You've set down some ground rules, you've returned to your faith and you're studying the Bible. I would encourage Samantha to go to church with you—just as she expects you to take her to cheerleading and other activities. She needs to get to know the Lord before she heads out on her own."

Pam looked at her watch. "We still have a few minutes before my next appointment. I sense that you have other concerns."

Aimee bowed her head and closed her eyes, praying for the right words to explain her situation. "I've carried a load of guilt since Steve died because I wasn't the kind of wife I should have been. I was eighteen when we married, and I got pregnant right away and had a lot of morning sickness. I was trying to become a homemaker, as well as a wife and mother, and I feel that I neglected Steve's needs."

Aimee swallowed hard and her voice drifted into a whisper. "My thoughts were all on myself and what I wanted. After our daughter was born, I couldn't bear the thought of intimate relations, so I slept in the nursery with Samantha. I've always felt guilty about neglecting Steve. I forget about it occasionally, but something always happens to remind me."

"And what happened this time to remind you?" Pam asked.

Aimee sat in the chair, her fingers clenched in her lap. She bit her lower lip, but finally drew a sharp breath. "Recently, I've met a man, the first one who's interested me since Steve's death. I don't know that anything will ever develop between us, but if it should, I don't want to fail him, too. He's trying to deal with his own past. If we should marry and I can't be the kind of wife I should be, it would be an added emotional blow to him."

"I wouldn't dwell too much on that situation," Pam said, understanding gleaming in her expressive eyes. "If you had ever shared your feelings with other women, you might find that it's pretty common after birth to avoid intimacy."

Pam's unexpected response confused Aimee, and she said, "I hadn't thought about that."

"After all, you were still young, and becoming pregnant and having a newborn is an emotional stress on any marriage," Pam said, and her voice was kind and reassuring. "Your husband was also young and perhaps stressed with the responsibilities of supporting a family. He probably understood your reluctance."

"Well, you've given me something new to consider," Aimee said and, knowing that her time was up, she stood. She shook hands with Pam. "Thank you. You've been very helpful. I feel much freer since I have discussed the situation with you."

"Always trust your concerns to God," Pam advised. "He always understands."

After her time with Pam, Aimee walked alone to the shore of the lake, and in spite of the cool breeze, she sat on a bench and looked out over the shimmering water. There was no one near, and she prayed aloud, *"Father, release me from the guilt that's hindered me for years. As I look back over the past, I don't believe Steve was unhappy with the situation between us. Maybe he understood my physical and emotional problems, or he probably would have been more demanding."*

She could almost feel the burden she'd carried for years leaving her heart. She felt cleansed, ready to use the mistakes of the past to become a better wife if she and Jacob ever had a future together.

Wanting to hear his voice, she checked her watch. He might be in the Siblings office at this hour, but wherever he was, he would probably answer his cell phone. She dialed his number, and he answered on the third ring.

"Aimee?" he asked quickly. "Are you all right?"

"Yes, more than all right," she said. "I'm sitting on the bank of the lake, looking out over a breath-taking mountain vista. I've been praying. I thought about you and decided to catch you if I could. Have you been to this camp?"

"A few times, but not since I was a boy. It's a great place and probably even better than when I camped there."

"The accommodations probably haven't changed since you were here," she said, laughing. "I didn't sleep much last night and missed my comfortable bed, but Erica says that's all part of a retreat."

"But you are having a good experience?" he asked.

"Yes, I am. The other women are warm and friendly. I've made lots of new friends, and the speaker is terrific. I had a short session with her this morning. I feel almost free."

"That's great," Jacob said. "I'll miss you at church tomorrow."

"I'd like to see you, too, but I'm glad I came here," Aimee told him. "I'm convinced that this retreat marks a turning point in my life, for I'm coming to terms with the past."

"I'm so glad! Give me a call when you get home."

"I will. We'll leave here tomorrow morning. Bye, Jacob."

Aimee remained at the lakeside for another half hour. Now that she no longer felt any guilt about her life with Steve, what else stood in the way of a deeper relationship with Jacob? Samantha's attitude was her biggest problem now. But what about Jacob? Although he'd shared his fear of rejection with her, why did she sense that it went much deeper than he'd let on?

Chapter Eleven

During the final session of the conference, most of the women, including Erica and Aimee, went forward to kneel and pray for renewal in their lives. Reluctant to leave the close fellowship they'd enjoyed over the weekend, Aimee and her roommates walked slowly back to the dormitory. Renewed in her spiritual walk, Aimee was eager to put what she'd experienced into her everyday situations.

When they were ready for bed, Aimee sat on a chair to file her nails. Erica lounged on the top bunk, eating an apple. Lori, sitting on her bunk, was brushing her long black hair. Aimee noticed that she was quieter, more serious than usual. She assumed that Lori, too, was thinking about the spiritual effect the conference had had on her life until Lori spoke hesitantly.

"Sisters, I've wanted to ask you something ever since you told me you were from Benton. I'm not one to gossip, but I'd like to have closure on something that has weighed on my mind for years. I'm speaking of an event that happened in Benton when I was living there."

Erica slashed a quick look toward Aimee. "As I told you, I wasn't living in Benton during those years," she said, "but you've made me curious. Go ahead."

"This might come across as gossip, but I've been sincerely concerned about the young man involved, and I've prayed for him over the years. I'd like to know what happened to him. Do you know a Jacob Mallory?"

Again Erica and Aimee exchanged quick glances, and the peaceful feeling that had infiltrated Aimee's heart and mind during the weekend fled. She was suddenly tongue-tied and waited for Erica to answer.

"I've known Jacob for several years," Erica said. "He attends the church we do, and he and I belong to the same singles group. He's the owner of a successful counseling service, and is well thought of in town."

"I'm very glad to hear that," Lori said sincerely.

"Well, go on," Erica said impatiently. "Why did you ask? Don't keep us in suspense."

Aimee wondered at Lori's manner—both anticipating and dreading to hear what concerned her. "So he's never married?" she asked.

"Not as far as I know," Erica said.

Seemingly groping for the right words, Lori said, "What about Megan Russell? Do you know her?"

Erica shook her head.

"I don't," Aimee said shortly, wishing Lori would stop asking questions and tell them what she knew. Still, Aimee had a hunch that she wasn't going to like what she heard. A wave of apprehension coursed through her body, and she watched her roommate anxiously, waiting for her to continue.

Lori took a deep breath, and said, "Well, here goes. Megan and Jacob attended the same high school I did. They dated steadily through high school. In her senior year, Megan got pregnant."

Aimee couldn't prevent the gasp that escaped her lips, and she assumed that her expression betrayed the shock Lori's words had caused. Lori looked at her curiously, but Aimee waved her hand for her to continue.

"Everybody thought Jacob was the father, but he flatly denied it and broke up with Megan. She hadn't been seeing anyone except him, so people tended to think he was guilty. But from what I knew of him, I thought there was more to the situation than what the general public knew."

Even Erica seemed shocked into silence, and in spite of her own chagrin, Aimee saw an element of humor in that fact.

Lori sighed heavily, and her expression was grim as she concluded, "I'm sure Jacob experienced a lot of shunning and ridicule before he went away to college and, and as far as I know, he didn't come back to Benton, not even to see his grandmother. I'm surprised to hear that he's living in Benton now."

"From what I know of Jacob, he isn't the kind of man to shirk his responsibility," Aimee said quietly. "If he was the father of that child, he would have said so."

"That's my opinion, too," Erica said. "And the fact that he came back to town and lived down his reputation is a lot to say in his favor."

"I agree with you," Lori said sincerely, "but Megan's family left Benton that summer, too. Two years later my father died, and my mother moved closer to her family. We haven't been back, although through the years, I've thought of Jacob. He was one of the most popular guys in our school, and it hurt me to see his reputation ruined like that. Sometimes I've wondered what he was doing, and if he'd gotten over Megan's betrayal. I thank God that Jacob lived down his bad reputation."

Aimee's faith in Jacob was strong enough that she was convinced he wasn't the father of

Megan's child, but she was crushed that Jacob had withheld this information from her. Still willing to defend his reputation, she said, "He's a good man. He and his grandmother are the founders of Substitute Siblings, an organization that helps children with problems."

"You can't imagine how pleased I am to hear that," Lori said.

Erica exchanged glances with Aimee again, and Erica said, "It must have taken a lot of strength to return and live down the stigma of his past."

Torn by conflicting emotions, Aimee said, "I can't imagine why we haven't heard about it."

"It does seem strange," Erica admitted. "But people who spread rumors will soon find another victim. Besides, he's done so much good in Benton that his friends would be quick to put down any gossip about him."

"You've taken a load off my mind," Lori said. "Off and on over the years, I've thought about Jacob. When I come to Benton in a few months, I hope to see him."

"He's a member of the committee planning the bicentennial," Aimee said, "so you'll have that opportunity."

"Be sure and tell him I said hello. No, on second thought, if you tell him that, he would know I'd been talking about him." Lori yawned. "I've got a long trip tomorrow, so I'd better get some sleep. It's been a blessing to share this conference with the two of you."

As she settled into bed, Aimee's thoughts about the conference faded into the background. Her rededication at the lake seemed a long time ago, and her thoughts of a future with Jacob plummeted. Why hadn't he told her about Megan Russell? Was it possible that he *was* the father of her child and hadn't accepted the responsibility?

Aimee spent a restless night and was exhausted when she slid behind the steering wheel of her car the next morning and started the drive back to Benton.

Erica and Aimee chatted aimlessly about the conference for the first fifty miles. When they stopped for gas, Erica took the wheel as they headed out on the road again. "We might as well talk about it," she said as she picked up speed on the four-lane highway.

Aimee didn't have to ask what she was talking about, for she knew that Jacob had been on both their minds all morning.

"I don't know how I can face him without letting him know what we've learned," Aimee said.

"Just how involved are your feelings toward Jacob?" Erica said with a sharp glance in Aimee's direction.

Grimly, Aimee responded, "They're deep enough that I was awake most of the night wondering why he hadn't told me about Megan Russell."

"That's what I figured," Erica said, a resigned look on her face. "Although I'm pleased at the change in you the past couple of months, I can't help be sorry that I ever invited you to the singles group."

"Don't feel that way. No matter what happens between Jacob and me, I'm not sorry, so don't feel responsible," Aimee assured her. "Your prodding was what I needed to understand how to deal with Samantha's maturing. With or without Jacob, I'm developing my own life."

They had to slow down for highway repairs, but when Erica was on smooth road again, Aimee continued, "And it's worth a lot to be in close fellowship with God. That's something I've really missed in my life." Aimee was silent for a few moments, thinking about her conversations with Jacob. "When he told me about his engagement and that the girl left him for another man, why didn't he complete the story and tell me what else had happened?"

Erica shook her head in concern. "I wonder if she married this other guy. I suppose one reason Megan and Jacob aren't still front-page news in Benton is because her family moved before the child was born, and they haven't been in town as a constant reminder of what happened."

"I feel so sorry for Jacob's having to live with this for so long," Aimee said.

"Has he avoided serious relationships because he's guilty of refusing to recognize his own child?" Erica wondered aloud. "Or is he afraid to trust another woman with his heart?" She shook her head in confusion. "It's a mystery to me."

"Either way, his life hasn't been easy," Aimee said.

Although they discussed Jacob off and on during their return to Benton, nothing eased the burden in Aimee's heart. When she pulled into her driveway, she still didn't have any clear direction as to how she should approach Jacob with this new knowledge. Was it better never to let him know what she'd learned at camp?

Normally, she would have called Jacob immediately to share more of her weekend experiences with him. She *wanted* to talk to him, but could she act as she had before she knew more about him?

Aimee hadn't called before Jacob left for the evening worship service at the church, and he thought surely she would have returned from the conference by the time he got home. But his caller ID didn't register that she had phoned, and he was worried. The road from Camp Serenity to Benton had many hills and curves, and he wondered if she'd had trouble. When he dialed her number, she answered on the first ring.

"So you're home," he said. "I hadn't heard from you, and I was worried."

"We got here about five o'clock, but I've been settling in."

"How was the conference?"

"Awesome! The campsite is beautiful. It's what I've needed for a long time. I'm glad Erica encouraged me to go."

"Can we have dinner together this week?"

"I don't know," she answered slowly. "I think Samantha has games this week, and I'll be taking her to them."

Trying to force his words into a teasing sound, he said, "Surely you'd have one free night. Are you trying to avoid me?"

"What makes you ask that?" she said quickly.

"I was only joking," he answered, trying to sound natural, but there was something different about Aimee. What could have happened during the weekend to cause her to be so cool toward him? "Maybe I can call in a few days?" he asked after several moments of silence.

"Sure. That will be fine," she answered, but it didn't sound as if she meant it.

Jacob laid the phone aside with an uneasy feeling. Something was wrong. He was tempted to go to Aimee's right away and confront her. No, he would wait for a few days. Maybe she was tired from the trip. And who knows what Samantha might have done to upset her?

Lacking enthusiasm, Jacob went about his work automatically for the next few days. Several times each evening, he'd pick up the telephone, wanting to call Aimee, but not knowing if he should.

By Thursday, he was desperate, and without giving her any warning, he drove by her house. The garage door was open, and her car was inside. He parked in front of the house. His heart skipped a beat when he lifted his hand to knock. What if she wouldn't talk to him?

Aimee opened the door and invited him in, but not with the warmth she had formerly shown toward him.

"Am I interrupting anything?"

"No. Samantha is spending the night with her friend Madison. Tomorrow is an off day for students. The teachers and staff have in-service meetings."

He watched her closely as they went into the family room. He hoped that she would sit on the couch, so he could sit beside her. Instead she sat in a lounge chair, so he took a chair close to hers.

"I had a note from Mrs. Slater praising you for what you've done for Chloe," he said, hoping to ease the chilly atmosphere that seemed to surround them.

"I haven't done as much as I want to," Aimee admitted, "but I called Chloe this evening, and we're having lunch together Saturday. I wish Samantha would accept my Siblings work. If she didn't completely ignore the situation, it would make my time with Chloe so much easier. Samantha apparently thinks that if she ignores what I'm doing, it isn't happening."

Aimee seemed to be babbling, perhaps to forestall any more invitations, and as she talked, Jacob realized more than ever that it was all about Samantha. Was she really that focused on he daughter still, or had something changed between them?

When she paused momentarily, he said softly, he said, "What's wrong, Aimee?"

She looked away.

"Have I offended you in some way?" Jacob asked.

She turned her head and met his eyes directly. "I don't know."

"What do you mean, 'you don't know'?"

Awkwardly, she cleared her throat, stirred uneasily in her chair, and eyed him with a grim expression. She took a deep breath and spoke tersely. "We shared a room at the conference with Lori Alexander. She used to live in Benton and graduated from Paramount High School. Do you remember her?"

He shook his head. "The name isn't familiar."

"Alexander is her married name."

"Then I may know her. But I don't understand what this has to do with us." The expression in her eyes alarmed him, and he spoke more sharply than he wanted to. "If you have something to tell me, spit it out already."

"Very well." Aimee stood and crossed to the window. With her back to him, she said, "She told us more about the situation between you and Megan Russell than you had bothered to tell me. She wasn't gossiping, she was sincerely concerned about how you had coped with the outcome of your broken relationship with Megan. She didn't believe you were the father of Megan's child."

Jacob was momentarily stunned, blaming himself for not sharing this information with her first. Why hadn't he told Aimee the whole story? "But do you believe that I was?" he asked, and his body tensed as he waited for her answer.

She turned slowly. "I don't want to believe it. But why didn't you tell me? It makes me wonder what else I don't know about you."

Hurt that she didn't trust him, Jacob said bitterly, "Have you been completely honest with me about your own past? I don't think you've told me everything, either. I believe you've held back information about your marriage that could affect us in the future."

"I told you everything I can tell you," Aimee said in a voice that was sharper than she'd intended it to be.

"Then we're right back where we started. Excuse me for bothering you tonight," he said. "I should have called first."

Although he knew he might be ruining his future with Aimee, Jacob stood up and walked out of the house. He had hoped that Aimee would stop him from leaving, but when she didn't, he drove away, stunned and miserable.

"Well, Mallory," he declared in disgust. "You've messed up for good this time. You were too concerned over your own petty hurts to consider how Aimee would feel when she learned about Megan."

Why hadn't he known that he couldn't keep that past situation from Aimee? He knew her well enough now to realize that she would have readily accepted his innocence in the affair with Megan without any questions.

Now—just as he realized that he had fallen in love with her—he'd lost her, and he had no one to blame but himself.

Chapter Twelve

Aimee was stunned by Jacob's reaction to what she'd told him. She had expected him to deny that he had fathered Megan's child. Had his anger indicated he was guilty, or was he hurt because she had doubted him?

All week she had questioned whether she should just forget what Lori had said and continue her friendship with Jacob. But she knew she would never forget it, and she couldn't spend the rest of her life wondering if Jacob was guilty. If Jacob had fathered that child, she had to know. It would break her heart if he admitted he had neglected his duty to the mother and child, but relationships must be built on truth and trust.

She slumped in a chair and wrung her hands in frustration. Her disappointment was too deep for tears. After avoiding male companionship for years, she thought she'd finally found a man she could respect. A man she could trust. Could she have been that wrong?

Aimee was still awake when the phone rang at one o'clock, and she nearly dropped the receiver when she saw that the call was from Mercy Hospital.

"Mrs. Blake," a compassionate voice answered her feeble hello. "Your daughter, Samantha, has just been admitted to the E.R."

"What happened? Is she okay?"

"Her injuries aren't critical, but she was involved in a car wreck on a county road. Her examination isn't complete."

"I'll be there right away," Aimee said and hung up the phone. She quickly dialed Erica's number.

Erica answered sleepily on the fifth ring. "Hey, Erica, Samantha has been in a wreck and is in the hospital. I'm shaking so bad I don't think I should be driving. Will you take me?"

"Of course! I'll dress right away. We'll go in my car. Meet me out front."

In less than ten minutes they were on their way to the hospital. "What happened?" Erica said as soon as Aimee got in the car.

"I don't know. I was so upset that all I could think of was getting to Samantha. She's been in an automobile accident, but the woman who called said that her condition didn't seem to be critical."

"Wasn't she staying with Madison tonight?"

"She was supposed to be at Madison's," Aimee responded grimly. "But I didn't check with Mrs. Toney to be sure it was all right. I have a suspicion now that I should have."

Not Madison's mother, but Jennifer's parents, Mr. and Mrs. Nibert, met them in the E.R. waiting room.

Wondering why they were there, Aimee asked, "What happened?"

"Nothing I'm proud of, you can be assured of that," Mr. Nibert said in an angry voice. "The three girls were out driving in Jennifer's car. I'll quickly relieve your mind by saying that none of them are seriously hurt, but Jennifer totaled the car. It's a miracle that all three of them weren't killed."

"Why would Mrs. Toney let the girls go out this time of night?" Aimee questioned. "Besides, I didn't know Jennifer was spending the night with Madison, too."

"Mr. and Mrs. Toney aren't home," Jennifer's mother said, flashing an apprehensive glance toward her husband. "They were called away suddenly to a funeral. All three of our daughters deceived us. Madison told her parents that she would spend the night with Samantha. You thought that Samantha would be at Madison's home. We knew that Jennifer would be with Madison, but we didn't know her parents were away."

Bristling with indignation, Mr. Nibert said, "This is it! I'm not buying Jennifer another car. If she wants one, she'll pay for it herself. Then she might understand that it isn't a toy."

He paced the floor, too angry to stand still.

"Have you seen Jennifer?" Aimee asked.

"Yes, and you can see Samantha," Mrs. Nibert said. "Go down the hall and someone will take you to her."

"Is Jennifer all right?" Erica inquired, and Aimee waited for the answer before she went to Samantha.

"She has a broken leg and some cuts and bruises," Mrs. Nibert answered. "We don't know about internal injuries yet."

"Did they hit anyone else?" Erica asked.

"No, it was a one car accident," Mr. Nibert said. "Jennifer was driving too fast and lost control on a curve. I'm sorry that Samantha was injured."

Aimee's face blanched at the thought of what could have happened. "It's Samantha's fault as well. She knows I wouldn't approve of the three of them spending the night alone or cruising on country roads in the middle of the night. Do you know how badly she's hurt?"

Mr. Nibert shook his head. "They wouldn't tell me."

A nurse motioned to Aimee and directed her to the cubicle where Samantha lay with her eyes closed. A nurse was installing an IV pump when Aimee entered the room.

Frightened at the white, strained face of her daughter, Aimee whispered, "How is she?"

"Her left arm is broken below the elbow, and she has a nasty cut on her leg. Her vitals are excellent, though, so she's going to be all right." The nurse moved a chair close to the gurney. "You can sit here until the doctor comes in."

Aimee looked at the equipment connected to Samantha's body, monitoring the blood pressure and pulse. She lowered her head into her hands and thanked God for protecting her daughter, yet dark images filtered into her consciousness as she thought how easily Samantha could have been killed. How could she have gone on without her?

Overcome by guilt, she thought again of how she had failed Steve. She'd allowed her daughter to become deceitful. If she'd been the right kind of mother, Samantha wouldn't be turning out the way she was.

She swallowed the sobs that rose in her throat, but she couldn't stop tears from slipping under her eyelids. So deep was her grief that she didn't hear anyone enter the cubicle until she felt a hand on her shoulder. She looked up quickly expecting to see the doctor, but was surprised to see Jacob.

She stood up quickly and walked into his outstretched arms. "How did you know?" she asked.

"Erica called me as soon as you told her about Samantha."

"She shouldn't have done that," Aimee said without much conviction in her voice.

"Oh, but she should have." He nestled her head on his shoulder, and peace flooded through Aimee's being. Everything would be all right now that Jacob was with her. No matter what he'd done in the past, she knew he was there for her now.

"How is she?"

"She has a broken arm. The doctor hasn't been in, but the nurse assured me that she doesn't have any life-threatening injuries." Although it felt like leaving a warm room to step into a freezer, she moved out of his arms.

Jacob encouraged her to sit down, and he knelt on the floor beside her and held her hand. "Want to talk about it?"

"I failed at being a mother again. Samantha told me she was spending the night with Madison, which was true. What she didn't tell me was that Madison's parents were away for the night, *and* that Jennifer was also at the sleepover."

Jacob cupped Aimee's chin in his fingers and turned her face toward him. "It was not *your* fault.

Believe me, it was not your fault." Grinning, he said, "Repeat after me, 'It was not my fault.'"

She shook her head. "I have to shoulder most of the blame. I should have checked with Mrs. Toney as I usually do."

"Samantha *lied* to you, and I'm sure you've never taught her to lie," he insisted. "She chose to do something she knew you wouldn't approve."

Her eyes filled with tears. "But she could have been killed! Madison's parents were called away unexpectedly, and Madison told her that she would spend the weekend with Samantha. They know that Madison is always welcome at our home, so they didn't okay the visit with me."

"So both girls were telling half truths."

"Yes, which, in my opinion, is still lying. Neither the Toneys nor I knew Jennifer would be with them. I don't know the details, but they decided to take a drive. Jennifer was driving too fast and lost control. Her father is very angry, and I have a feeling he's going to put a stop to Jennifer's waywardness."

"So, good may come out of the situation, which might be the reason God allowed it to happen." Grinning widely, Jacob added, "I don't know the Niberts, but I saw a very angry man bawling out his wife in the waiting room. Apparently he'd relegated his paternal responsibilities to his wife, and she's been too lenient with Jennifer."

"I agree with him, but he should have taken more interest in his daughter before this," Aimee replied. "Best I can tell from what Jennifer says—he's hardly ever at home. Maybe this will bring their family closer together."

Returning to Aimee's major concern, Jacob said, "This accident resulted from the actions of many people. Very little of the blame, if any, can be laid at your door. Promise me that you will stop feeling guilty."

A moan escaped Samantha's lips and Aimee hurried to the bed. Samantha's eyes were still closed but she sat up and started to get out of bed.

"No, dear," Aimee said. "You can't get up."

Samantha opened her eyes and pushed Aimee's hand away. Jacob went to the other side of the gurney.

"Samantha, lie still," he said calmly but firmly. "You're hooked up to several machines, and you'll injure yourself if you don't lie still."

Samantha's eyes wavered in his direction, and she quieted under his restraining hand on her arm. Aimee's worried eyes met Jacob's, and he said, "Certain medicines have this effect on many people, especially those who aren't used to taking a lot of medication."

Gently, Jacob continued to encourage Samantha to lie still, and she was quiet again when the E.R. doctor came in soon afterward. He checked the computerized report the nurse had left behind, monitored Samantha's pulse and listened to her heart and lungs. He showed Aimee and Jacob the X-rays of Samantha's arm, indicating where the break was.

"She's okay, but we'll admit her for the rest of the night to allow time for some of the swelling to go down. The orthopedic surgeon will take care of her early tomorrow. Don't worry. You can see that it's a clean break, and she should heal quickly. She'll be discharged by midmorning."

"May I stay with her?" Aimee asked.

He nodded. "Room 215. I'm sure she'll want her mother with her when she comes to herself."

When the orderly came to wheel Samantha out of the E.R. unit, Aimee walked to the waiting room with Jacob. Erica came to them at once and hugged Aimee.

"Had a rough time, huh?"

Aimee smiled. "Do I look that bad?"

"I've seen you look better," Erica joked. "But if you're able to smile, Samantha must be all right."

Jacob reported what the doctor had said.

"I'll stay the rest of the night with her," Aimee said, "but there isn't any reason for either of you to stay. I'll have to take off a few days from school."

"Do you want me to call the principal?" Erica said.

"Please."

"I'll phone early," Erica promised. "Also, when they discharge her, call me, and I'll come for you. I don't have to work tomorrow."

"I'll pick them up, Erica," Jacob said.

"It's my day off, but you have to work," Erica objected.

He shook his head. "I'm my own boss, and I don't have any appointments tomorrow that can't be postponed," Jacob insisted. "I'll bring them home. You know my cell-phone number, Aimee, so let me know when Samantha will be released."

He pulled Aimee into a friendly embrace, and over his shoulder, Aimee's eyes met Erica's, who smiled, lowered her left eyelid in a wink and gave her thumbs-up. Aimee tried to frown at her friend, but her heart was too full of thankfulness and peace to be annoyed at anyone right now. Not even Samantha.

Jacob drove away from the hospital knowing that his relationship with Aimee had undergone significant changes tonight. His feelings for her differed greatly from his emotions for Megan. He supposed that had been a case of puppy love, and that he had been hurt because Megan wanted someone else more than she wanted him. Well, he was thirty-four years old now, and it was way past time for him to be concerned about rejection.

Jesus had been rejected over and over, yet He had persevered and hadn't closed His heart to other people because His own family and peers wouldn't accept Him.

Right from the first, Jacob had been drawn to Aimee. He believed she was interested in him, but did they have too many emotional scars from the past to consider anything beyond friendship? Plus, anyone who married Aimee would always be competing with Samantha for Aimee's love. He wasn't sure he wanted to play second fiddle.

Jacob knew that he'd made a mistake when he hadn't told her the complete story about his involvement with Megan. He should have told her before she learned the information secondhand. But now he thought they could get past it. With God's help they could get past anything.

Samantha woke up when a nurse entered the room to check her vitals. She looked around, dazed, and her eyes focused on Aimee.

"Mom! Where are we?"

"In the hospital."

"What happened?" Then she closed her eyes. "Oh, I remember. We went around a bend. The car started spinning like a top. There was a big crash. That's all I remember. I ache all over. Am I hurt bad?"

"You have a broken arm."

"What about Jen and Madison?"

"Madison had a few cuts, but she didn't have to stay in the hospital. Her grandmother came and picked her up. Jennifer wasn't so fortunate. She has a broken leg and possible internal injuries."

"Well, it's her own fault," Samantha said, frowning. "Madison and I tried to get her to slow down."

"She might have been driving too fast, but don't blame anyone except yourself for your injuries," Aimee said sharply. "No one made you get in the car with Jennifer. Perhaps this isn't the time to say I told you so, but I'm very disappointed in you. You know I wouldn't want you girls to spend the night alone."

"It was one of those crazy things that just happened. We thought it would be a blast to spend the night alone. Till Jen got the crazy idea to go driving."

"Have you listened to one single word I've said?" Aimee asked. "Don't blame Jennifer for *your* actions. You got into her car of your own free will."

Tears squeezed out of Samantha's eyes, and Aimee was sorry she had spoken harshly. The only justification for her anger was that she still hadn't gotten over the shock of possibly losing her daughter. She had to make Samantha more responsible for her actions.

Fortunately, the orthopedic surgeon came in at that time and forestalled further comment. He examined Samantha and asked the nurse who accompanied her to call for an orderly to take her to surgery. Samantha cast a fearful glance at her mother.

"Will you stay with me?"

"I'm afraid that isn't possible, love, but the doctor and nurses will take good care of you. I'll be here in the room when you get back." She bent over the bed and kissed Samantha. "I love you, Samantha. No matter what."

"You'll have time to go to the cafeteria for breakfast," the nurse said.

Aimee walked beside the gurney until they came to the elevator, where she kissed Samantha again. Instead of eating breakfast, she stepped outside the hospital to call Erica and Jacob.

Samantha had been given an injection so she wouldn't be aware when the doctor set her arm, and she was still woozy when Jacob helped her into his car. She dozed all the way home, and he stayed at the house until Aimee put her to bed. Samantha either didn't realize that he was helping, or had decided to ignore him.

When she was settled, Jacob said to Aimee, "Now it's your turn to get some rest. I'm leaving, but I'm as close as a phone call. If I don't hear, I'll call later."

He leaned forward and kissed Aimee's forehead and caressed her cheek with his gentle hand. "I'm here for you, Aimee. Don't forget that."

Aimee walked to the window and watched him drive away, wondering what he meant by his last statement. She knew the time was fast approaching when she had to admit how important Jacob Mallory was to her future. She only prayed that she wouldn't have to choose between Jacob and Samantha to find happiness.

Chapter Thirteen

Aimee was still sleeping when Mrs. Toney telephoned.

"How's Samantha?" she asked.

"She was discharged from the hospital this morning, and she's been sleeping since we got home. The doctor says she's fine. It was a straight break and should heal quickly."

"I'm glad to hear it. I want to apologize for Madison's part in this deception. My sister died quite suddenly. We've always been close and, in my grief, I didn't call to see if it was all right for Madison to stay with you. I had no reason to think she would lie to me."

"Madison is always welcome here. And as far as I'm concerned, all the girls are equally at fault. I even blame myself for giving Samantha too much freedom, but it won't happen again."

"That's why I called. Mr. Nibert and I had a long talk this morning. He says that if Jennifer gets another car, she's buying it, and we both agreed to put our daughters on a strict schedule. They're not staying overnight anywhere except at home until school is out, and they'll be on probation all summer. We hope you'll agree to these restrictions."

"I certainly will. I intend to put Samantha on a short leash, but it will be so much easier if all of the parents agree on their punishment. By the way, how is Jennifer?"

"She has several broken ribs, a broken leg, a punctured lung and a wound on her arm, as well as a slight concussion. She'll be in the hospital for several days. Her father said that she's more upset about a possible scar on her arm than she is anything else."

"Sounds like Jennifer," Aimee agreed. "We were all blessed that it wasn't worse."

"That's certainly true."

"I'm willing to go along with the ground rules you and Mr. Nibert have agreed on," Aimee assured her.

Perhaps Samantha also felt that she was fortunate to avoid a more serious injury, for she didn't argue when she heard about the restrictions.

When Jacob stopped by Monday evening,

Samantha was even amiable, if not friendly. Soon after he arrived, Samantha asked to be excused, told Jacob good-night and went to her room, saying that she needed to catch up on her homework before she started back to school.

Jacob lifted his eyebrows and winked at Aimee as they listened to Samantha's footsteps on the stair treads.

Grinning, Aimee said quietly, "Let's hope this lasts."

When they went into the family room, Jacob took her hand and led her to the couch. He put his arm around her shoulders, and she nestled close to him.

"Now, it's time for me to tell you what I should have told you weeks ago," he said regretfully. "I'm so sorry you had to learn from someone else why I broke up with Megan. I lived through a bad six months in this town when Megan's pregnancy became obvious, and I've never gotten over it. I was naive and hadn't even realized she was going to have a baby until my friends started kidding me about it."

She leaned her head back and peered into his eyes. "Jacob, you don't have to tell me anything. I shouldn't have doubted you."

He shook his head decisively. "I don't want any secrets between us. I'd dated Megan for almost three years, and I suppose I loved her in a youthful sort of way. I was really hurt when I knew she hadn't been faithful to me."

Aimee could sense the pain in his voice. He paused and swallowed with difficulty before he continued. "We had never been intimate, so there was no way the child was mine. Megan wouldn't give the name of the father, and I didn't really want to know, because if the news ever got out who the other man was, I figured I'd be the laughingstock of Benton. I wasn't mature enough to take that kind of ridicule, so I left Benton to go to college, never intending to live here again."

"Why did you come back?" Aimee asked.

"Well, for one thing, Gran was here, and I felt I needed to take care of her."

Aimee giggled slightly, and Jacob said, "I know, it's ironic. Gran can take care of herself, and even thinks she still has to look after me. But someday, it may be different, and I'll be here if she ever needs me."

"She's an amazing woman," Aimee agreed, glad that she'd thought of something to lighten the moment.

"But it was more than Gran that brought me back," he said. "I'd never felt right about taking the coward's way out. So I took my own counseling advice and came home to live down my past reputation."

"Did it take very long?" she asked, covering his hand with hers.

"It was a couple of years before I sensed that some of my acquaintances no longer thought about the situation. And the fact that I've been able to build up a good practice in spite of the past has been encouraging."

"You've never heard from Megan?"

"No. I stopped seeing her immediately, and after a few weeks when she finally learned that I wouldn't have anything else to do with her, she stopped calling me." He paused a moment. "Her betrayal killed any love I ever had for her, but I still feel badly that I abandoned her. She probably needed friends then."

"You shouldn't blame yourself," Aimee was quick to defend his actions. "Whoever fathered that child should be the one to feel guilty. You don't have any idea who she could have been seeing?"

"Not a hint. She wouldn't tell me anything. Perhaps it was non-Christian for me not to help her. Today, I might make such a sacrifice, but I was too young then to make far-reaching decisions."

"Do you know anything about the child?" Aimee asked.

He shook his head. "Megan left Benton before I did. Gran heard that she went to stay with her grandmother in Tennessee and that the baby was born there. Her parents sold their property and moved away from Benton, too. I haven't heard anything else, and I hope I never hear from her again."

"It seems to me that you did the right thing in moving back to Benton," Aimee assured him.

"Yes," he agreed. "Time has proven that, but it was a difficult decision to make."

"You accused me of not being completely open with you about my past," she said, "and you're right. Although it's embarrassing I'm going to tell you one of the things that's bothered me. After meeting with Pam Baker at the conference, I've realized that the fear that has shadowed my life was a normal reaction to my pregnancy."

Jacob must have noticed her heightened coloring, for he said, "Don't hesitate to tell me anything. I won't be judgmental."

"I know that," she said, "and I want you to know, although it's difficult to talk about. I've told you that I got pregnant within two months of our marriage. I was only eighteen years old, had morning sickness and all the discomfort that goes with it. I was miserable, both physically and emotionally, the whole nine months. Consequently, I avoided the intimacies of marriage as much as possible."

Aimee could not sit beside Jacob as she discussed the intimate details of her life with Steve, so she walked to the window. The outside lights shone brightly on the little gazebo, and Aimee focused on it as she collected her thoughts in an effort to continue.

"After Samantha was born, I moved into another bedroom. After Steve died, I felt very guilty that I'd neglected him and hadn't been the kind of wife I should have been." She looked away from him, hoping that she had succinctly conveyed the situation to Jacob without adding further details. "I decided I wasn't the type of person who should be married."

Jacob left the couch and put his arm around her, and turned her to face him. "I don't believe that for a minute," he said.

Aimee experienced an unusual tremor of excitement when he lowered his face to hers. She relaxed in his embrace as she raised her face to meet his sweet kiss. When he released her lips, Aimee exhaled a long sigh of contentment and rested her head on his shoulder.

His hand smoothed her hair as he spoke. "Until I talk to my grandparents and learn more about my father and why he abandoned my mother and me, I can't say the things I want to say, or discuss a future with you. My family background could change everything, but believe me, you would be a good wife to any man, so don't worry about that."

She couldn't tell him that her reaction to his

embrace was totally different from anything she had felt for Steve. The years had made a difference. If only she had listened to her parents' plea that she was too immature to get married, her life might have taken another turn.

Aimee stayed home with Samantha for two days, but after a visit to the doctor, although she would have to carry her arm in a sling for two weeks, Samantha was released to return to school. When she protested about the sling, the doctor said, "You'll have less pain than if you let your arm dangle at your side."

"Mom," Samantha protested the next morning, "this cast and sling look gross. Let me stay home until I'm completely well. Madison and Jen won't be there."

"Jennifer may have to miss several weeks of school. But why won't Madison be there?"

"Her parents went to the memorial service for the sister who died. They took Madison with them. I can't carry a backpack with this sling."

Although she, too, was worried that Samantha might find school difficult, Aimee said, "I'm sure there will be someone willing to help you."

"I don't know. The other kids are jealous of Jen, Madison and me. They say we're stuck-up."

Aimee didn't doubt that Samantha and her

friends were cliquish and conceited, but she didn't comment. However, her heart ached for Samantha, who looked scared when she got out of the car in front of the school. Aimee would gladly have helped Samantha inside, but she wouldn't welcome her mother carrying her books either. Aimee went to work breathing a silent prayer that God would send someone to help Samantha through the day.

The day was hectic for Aimee as she tried to catch up on the work that had piled up on her desk while she'd been away. Samantha was in the back of her mind all day long. When she stopped in front of the school, Samantha waited for her, and to her surprise, Chloe Spencer stood beside her holding Samantha's book bag.

"Why, hello, Chloe," Aimee said as she opened the door for Samantha.

"Thanks for helping out," Samantha said to Chloe.

"You're welcome. See ya, Mrs. Blake. I've got to catch my bus."

"I'll call you in a few days," Aimee said as Chloe hurried away.

Aimee monitored the constant flow of traffic in front of the school, and slowly eased into the line. "How'd your day go?" she asked when they were out of the school traffic zone.

"Not good! My arm hurt all day. And I've got tons of homework."

"Didn't anything good happen?" Aimee asked.

"Yeah. One of the guys carried my books for me. But he had track practice after school." Reluctantly, she added, "Chloe carried my backpack to the car." Changing the subject abruptly, she added, "I'm tired."

"I'm sure you are, but tomorrow will be easier."

Aimee hoped that this incident would soften Samantha's attitude toward Chloe, but she didn't intend to comment on it. If Samantha wanted to participate in her activities with Chloe, she would have to take the initiative. She couldn't be forced to be kind to Chloe.

Jacob dozed through the bicentennial meeting as report after report was read. He was glad when they handed out a list of the out-of-town people who expected to attend. He skimmed the list to see how many of them he recognized. He sat upright in his chair, and his heart skipped a beat when he read a name that still had the power to distress him. Megan Russell.

Why did she have to return now? And just when he'd met Aimee and was looking forward to a future with her! What would Aimee think if she knew that Megan was coming to the bicentennial? Should he tell her or wait and hope that he wouldn't have to see Megan at all?

His thoughts were interrupted when the chairman said, "We've saved the most interesting business until last." He took the wrapping off of a large package. "The plaque honoring Mr. Harwood was delivered today. I'm very pleased with it, and I hope you will be, too." He steadied the bronze plaque on the table and read ponderously, "David Lee Harwood, beloved teacher, administrator, family man and civic leader of Benton."

Jacob leaned forward to see the rest of the printing on the plaque, which included a quotation by Robert F. Kennedy. Harwood's birth and death dates, as well as a list of his more memorable achievements, were inscribed in smaller print.

"Did Mr. Harwood have a family?" Jacob asked, to show interest in the dedication, although his mind raced with thoughts of the impending arrival of Megan.

"His wife and two children live here," the chairman said, "and they'll be accepting the plaque."

Jacob stood up. "If that's all the business, I'll have to leave. I have an early appointment in the morning."

But Jacob didn't get much rest that night. His mind was on overdrive as he considered what Megan's return might do to his relationship with

Aimee. Was it possible that he could avoid Megan completely? There would be a lot of people in Benton that day, and unless she sought him out, it was unlikely they would meet. And if they did meet they might not even recognize each other.

Jacob had destroyed all of Megan's pictures, and he barely remembered what she looked like. Her photo was in the school yearbook, but he didn't know where his copy was. Wasn't the fact that he'd forgotten her physical features an indication that any feelings he had once held for her were gone forever?

Since he'd been too busy all day to check his e-mail, Jacob accessed his account on his PC as soon as he got home. He skimmed messages about business that required attention, but when he saw a post from Andrew Mallory, he quickly opened the file.

Jacob, his grandfather had written, we plan to leave Florida June 15 and will stop in your town two or three days later. We will call in advance to let you know what time we'll arrive in Benton. Will it be convenient for us to stop at that time?

Jacob started to reply, but he hesitated. Perhaps he should wait and talk the visit over with Gran. She would probably want to invite the Mallorys to stay overnight in her home, but on second thought, since he didn't know the nature of his grandparents' visit, he decided to let them make what arrangements they wanted.

He quickly typed a return message. As far as I know now, those dates are convenient for me. My maternal grandmother lives nearby, and I'll want you to meet her, too.

Jacob would have liked to talk over the upcoming visit with Gran or Aimee, but it was past midnight, and both of them were probably asleep. He hadn't felt so uneasy since the days he was confronted with Megan's deception. It was a few weeks before his grandparents' visit, and he dreaded the wait.

As long as Samantha still had her arm in a cast, Aimee didn't want to leave her alone on Saturdays, but she didn't want to shirk her responsibilities to Chloe either. All day Friday, she thought often of how to approach Samantha without alienating her from Chloe. Chloe had continued to carry Samantha's book bag to the car each afternoon that week, and Samantha had thanked her, but she didn't talk about Chloe to Aimee.

On Saturday morning, Aimee said, "I promised Chloe I would help her make cookies for the reception after the spring chorale. I'm going to bring her over here for the afternoon."

Not looking at her mother, Samantha asked, "What kind of cookies are you going to make?"

"I'll help her make two kinds so her plate will have a variety. She needs to take four dozen cookies. What ones do you think will go over well with the students?"

"Everybody likes brownies."

"Those are easy to make," Aimee agreed. "We'll make a pan of those. What else?"

"What about the peanut-butter ones with a chocolate kiss on top?" Samantha suggested.

"Oh, you mean peanut blossoms! That would be a good choice—they're pretty cookies, as well as yummy. I'll call Chloe and tell her I'll come for her about one o'clock. Do you want to ride to her house with me?" Aimee invited.

"No."

"If you want to go along when I take her home, after we drop Chloe off at her house, we'll stop for burgers and fries."

"Okay," Samantha said, and Aimee smothered a grin. Samantha never turned down a visit to a fast-food restaurant.

Aimee had expected Samantha to stay in her room during the cookie baking, and she was surprised when she and Chloe returned to find Samantha in the family room watching television.

"Hi, Samantha," Chloe said. Aimee held her breath, hoping that Samantha wouldn't shun Chloe's natural friendliness.

"Hi back atcha," Samantha said. She turned off the TV and came into the kitchen. She went to the fridge and took out a can of pop.

"Want something to drink, Chloe?" Samantha asked.

"Not right now, but maybe later. I want to get started on the cookies. I know how to make Rice Krispies squares, but that's all. Grandma does all the baking."

"Mom and I used to make cookies together," Samantha said, and Aimee thought she noted a hint of nostalgia, or was it remorse? That was one of the first things Samantha had stopped doing with her mother.

"Maybe you can help me," Chloe suggested.

"Not much I can do with only one hand."

"We'll think of something," Aimee said. "If these sound good to you, Chloe, you can make brownies and peanut-butter cookies with chocolate kisses on them."

"Suits me," Chloe approved.

"Which one do you want to do first?" Aimee asked.

"Brownies," Chloe said promptly. "I've watched Grandma make them."

Aimee had made copies of the recipes in big print on the computer, and she handed the brownie recipe to Samantha.

"It will be easier for Chloe if you read the recipe aloud, step by step."

"Yes," Chloe agreed. "I'm nervous as all get-out. Face it—I may make a mess of things."

"You won't," Aimee assured her. "I've set out the flour, sugar and other ingredients and several bowls, a baking dish for the brownies and two cookie sheets," Aimee explained as she sat on a stool at the serving bar. "I'll be here for advice, but I want you to do everything."

Chloe turned on the faucet, soaped her hands and washed them thoroughly. "Well, here goes," she said. "So what do I do first, Samantha?"

"Spray the pan with shortening and dust the bottom lightly with flour," Samantha read.

Aimee watched as they went step by step through the recipe in perfect harmony until Chloe slid the baking pan into the oven. "What's next?"

"The brownies will be baked by the time you have the first sheet of drop cookies ready for the oven," Aimee told her.

"Say, Chloe," Samantha asked, "can I put the chocolate kisses on the cookies? I can do that with one hand."

"Yeah. The picture shows the kisses right in the middle of the cookie. My hands are kinda shaky. I'd probably stick them on every which way."

"Don't forget, you don't put the kisses on until

the cookies have baked fifteen minutes or so," Aimee cautioned.

"Ten minutes, and then put them back in the oven to bake three to five more minutes," Samantha corrected as she checked the recipe for the peanut blossoms.

After the cookies were baked and while they cooled enough to pack, Aimee helped the girls clean the countertops and put the dishes in the washer. "Do you want a tray or plate to hold the cookies when you take them to school?"

Chloe shook her head. "Grandma has a pretty tray that she's had a long time. I want to use it. That way, she'll have a part in this."

"Then we'll put these in a plastic container to keep them fresh until the chorale," Aimee said. "Is your grandmother going with you?"

"Yes, unless her arthritis acts up."

"If you need a ride, let me know," Aimee said. "Now we'd better get you home before your grandmother starts worrying about you."

"She never worries when I'm with you." Chloe took a phone from her pocket. "I'll call and tell her I'll be home soon. That way, she'll know when to start supper."

Samantha shuffled her feet. "Why can't Chloe eat burgers and fries with us, Mom?"

Without flicking an eyelash, Aimee said,

"That's a good idea, and we could buy a burger plate for you to take home to your grandmother. Tell her not to prepare anything for either of you."

Aimee credited part of this change of heart on Samantha's part to the fact that she and her two best friends weren't being allowed to hang out together as much as they used to, and their phone conversations were limited, too. No doubt Samantha was lonely. But whatever had caused the change, Aimee was overjoyed to know that Samantha's attitude toward Chloe had improved considerably.

That problem seemed to be partially settled, but would Samantha ever accept Jacob?

Chapter Fourteen

"Hi, Jacob," Aimee said when he answered his phone. "Seems like it's been a long time since we've had any time together."

"Tell me about it! I wanted to ask you out, but I know how busy you are."

"I'm going to the school chorale on Tuesday evening to hear Chloe sing. Would you like to go with me? Samantha will be there because she and Madison are ushers. They have to be at the school early, so Mrs. Toney is going to drop by and get Samantha."

"I do want to see the program, and Chloe needs all of the support she can get. Besides, I've missed seeing you. I'll stop by and pick you up. Does Chloe need a ride to the chorale?"

"No, a neighbor is taking Chloe and her grand-mother. We should leave here soon after six.

There will probably be a crowd and parking will be difficult."

"I'll be there by six."

Aimee knew that by going to the chorale with Jacob, she was opening a door of conjecture about their relationship to many people she'd worked with in the educational system. But she didn't intend to lose any sleep over it.

On Tuesday evening, when she opened the door to his knock, Jacob pulled her into a slight embrace.

"I've missed you. How long has it been since I've seen you?"

"I was at church Sunday."

"That doesn't count."

He still had his arms around her, and Aimee realized she was content to lean on him. She looked into his expressive eyes, trying to determine what his feelings were toward her. "We have to leave or we'll be late," she said reluctantly.

"I know, but it's frustrating," Jacob said. "We've known each other three months, and I can count on one hand how much quality time we've had together."

"But both of us have obligations to others, and if I read my Bible correctly, that's the way it should be. Christians are supposed to put the needs of others above their own desires. I have my parents and Samantha. You have Gran and your clients. Both of us have the Siblings. But I truly believe that if we fulfill those obligations, God will give us time for ourselves."

"I know you're right, but I want to see you more often," Jacob said somewhat peevishly. "Let's go."

Madison and Samantha greeted them at the door of the auditorium. Samantha spoke politely to Jacob, and Aimee couldn't tell from her expression what she thought. The girls guided them to empty seats, and while they waited for the program to start, Aimee introduced Jacob to several of her co-workers, not surprised that many of them already knew him.

The chorale had a spring theme, and consisted of old songs, such as "In the Good Old Summertime," "Easter Parade," several classical selections and a medley of modern songs. Aimee was delighted when Chloe sang a short solo in one of the modern selections. Her eyes sought Aimee's as she sang, and Aimee realized that Chloe had deliberately kept this secret as a gift to her.

After the chorale, Jacob and Aimee hurried to the front of the auditorium to speak to Chloe. Her eyes were bright with happiness and she returned Aimee's hug.

"I was very proud of you," Aimee said.

"It made my day when our director asked me to sing. I owe it all to you," Chloe said softly.

"Oh, no. God gave you the voice."

"But I wouldn't have had the nerve to try out if you hadn't told me I could do it."

"And from now on," Jacob added, "you'll not be afraid to try new things. Aimee and I will keep in touch with you to be sure that you do."

Madison and Samantha joined them, accompanied by Mrs. Toney.

"Whoo-hoo! Chloe," Madison said. "Your song was super," and Samantha halfheartedly agreed. Although she knew she shouldn't even hint at the possibility, Aimee hoped that Chloe's acceptance in the choir might open the door for Samantha to befriend her.

"If you have other plans," Mrs. Toney said to Aimee, "I can drop Samantha off at home."

"That won't be necessary," Jacob said. "Aimee came with me—Samantha can ride home with us."

Samantha was silent most of the way home, and when they went in the house, she said, "Thanks for bringing me home, Mr. Mallory. See ya round! 'Night, Mom."

When Aimee went downstairs, Jacob smiled and lifted his brows significantly. But Aimee shrugged her shoulders. "I've learned that I can't outthink a teenager," she said quietly. "Her good behavior might be a lull before the storm, or a ploy to wheedle something out of me."

Jacob drew her into his arms. He pulled her head down on his shoulder and smoothed her hair with his hand. Aimee marveled at how safe she felt with him. She wanted to tell him that just being with him was comforting. But when she lifted her head to speak, he silenced her with a kiss.

When he released her lips after an endless moment, she murmured, "Thank you, Jacob."

She raised her eyes to find him watching her with a gaze as sweet as a caress. "Thank me for what?"

"For kissing me."

He laughed softly, and when he started to speak, she said, "No, let me get this said before I lose my nerve." She swallowed. "For several years I've doubted if I was capable of feeling—of sensing any kind of emotion, but I know better now. When you kiss me, I feel alive." She stopped short of explaining the depth to which he had stirred her emotions.

He kissed her again. "You've made me very happy tonight. I'll leave now, but one of these days we're going to have some time for ourselves, and I'll find the right words to tell you what you mean to me."

"Mr. Mallory," Samantha said when Jacob answered his phone. "This is Samantha Blake. Mom's birthday is the first day of June. She'll be thirty-five. Erica and Grammy are helping me plan a surprise dinner for her."

Jacob smiled. He didn't know if Aimee would be happy to have her daughter sharing such personal information, but the fact that Samantha was including him seemed to indicate that she was slowly accepting him as a part of Aimee's life. "Sound like a good thing to do," he said.

"If we have it on Saturday night, it will be more of a surprise."

"That's true. Sundays are busy, too," he commented.

"Well, I want to invite you. Can you make it?"

Without checking his calendar, Jacob didn't know if he already had a commitment for the first day of June, but if he did he'd cancel it. Obviously, Samantha was thawing in her attitude toward him, and he intended to capitalize on it. "I'm free that evening. What time?"

"At six."

"Sounds like you've got it all planned out," Jacob said.

"Erica is doing most of the work," Samantha admitted. "I've invited Chloe Spencer. Would you bring her with you? That would be seven of us. Erica says that's enough for the size of our dining-room table."

"I'll be glad to bring Chloe," Jacob agreed

readily. "It's thoughtful of you to do this for your mother."

"I know," she said complacently, and again Jacob stifled a shout of laughter. "But really it was Erica who suggested it. See ya."

Regardless of whose idea it had been originally, Jacob knew that Aimee would regard the dinner as a breakthrough in her relationship with Samantha, and Jacob was pleased with anything that made Aimee happy.

He gave a lot of thought to a gift. Deciding that flowers were always appropriate, he ordered a dozen pink roses. On Saturday night when he went to pick up Chloe, she answered his knock, holding a wrapped package and looking excited. "This is gonna be so fun," she said.

Mrs. Slater came to the door with the aid of a cane. "Thanks for stopping by for her," she said. With a fond look at Chloe, she added, "I've never seen her so excited. Your Substitute Siblings organization has made a change in her life."

"Thank you. That's the kind of comment I like to hear," he said.

"It's true," Mrs. Slater said. "I hear many good reports from people you've helped."

As they drove toward Aimee's home, Chloe chattered about events at school, and Jacob compared how quiet and timid she'd been when he and Aimee had first met her with how she was today. The association between Chloe and Aimee had been good for both of them.

Samantha met them at the door, held her fingers to her lips and hurried them into the family room. "Mom doesn't know that the two of you are here," she whispered. "She'll be totally freaked out."

Jacob figured that was probably an understatement considering Samantha's earlier reaction to Chloe and him.

A man, probably in his sixties, approached Jacob with outstretched hand. "I'm Ed Ross, Aimee's father. And you are…"

"Jacob Mallory, Aimee's friend. Erica introduced us a few months ago."

"Glad to meet you, Jacob. You'll meet my wife, Martha, soon. She and Erica are making last-minute preparations for our dinner."

Jacob introduced Chloe. "She and Aimee are paired together in Substitute Siblings."

Jacob heard a door close and Samantha stuck her head out into the hall. She looked around at them, her dark-lashed gray eyes bright with excitement.

"Here she comes," she said in a stage whisper. With one eye still on the hallway, she lifted her hands as if she were an orchestra leader. She pumped her arms. "Now!"

Their loud "Happy Birthday" brought Erica and

Martha from the dining room. In a strong bass voice, Ed started singing, "Happy birthday to you."

While they sang, Aimee moved from one to the other, hugging them. Since everyone else was being hugged, Aimee hugged Jacob, too, and throughout the dinner, he wondered how much Aimee's parents knew about their relationship.

"We'll eat first and open gifts later," Erica said. She took the floral box from the small table where Jacob had laid it. "Unless these should be in water."

"I just picked them up, but they're probably better off in some water."

Aimee lifted out the long-stemmed flowers and placed them in the vase Jacob handed her. "This is a gift from Gran," he added.

"How nice of her!" Aimee said. Erica took the flowers and placed them on the shelf of the bay window in the family room.

After the meal, Martha and Erica served cake and ice cream in the family room while Aimee opened the rest of her gifts. Her parents had bought her a denim suit. She received a gift certificate for a massage from Erica. Samantha had bought a set of hand and body lotions. Chloe squirmed in her seat, and her face flushed when Aimee started opening her gift—a knitted neck scarf her grandmother had made. While he watched Aimee's pleasure in the attention she was receiving, Jacob anticipated a time when he could buy many gifts for her.

Aimee was delighted that Jacob had been invited to the party, but she couldn't show the extent of her excitement because she didn't want her mother to get any ideas. But the fact that Samantha had invited both Chloe and Jacob, Aimee felt, was definitely a step in the right direction. Still, Aimee didn't know if Samantha was willing yet for anything more than friendship between her mother and Jacob.

And she didn't want her parents to have even a hint of how much she thought of him. Her mother was pretty shrewd, especially where her daughter was concerned, so she knew it would be hard to fool her. Plus, Jacob fit so well into the family gathering. He and her father had no difficulty finding a common thread of conversation, for it seemed that Jacob's grandfather had owned a farm where Jacob had spent most of his summers when he was a boy.

And she couldn't see a bit of condescension in Samantha's attitude toward Chloe, which made her wonder if they visited some at school. Jennifer was still unable to attend classes, and although she was much better, the doctor advised that she should avoid crowds for a few more weeks. Samantha talked to Jennifer frequently, and she had visited Jennifer at home a few times, but

Aimee thought that the breakup of the threesome for a few weeks was giving Samantha time to make new friends.

Jacob and Chloe left before the others, and Aimee walked to the door with them. She hugged Chloe and thanked her for coming, asking her to thank Mrs. Slater for the gift. Jacob squeezed her hand. "See you at church tomorrow," he said.

"Jacob seems like a fine man," Martha said as soon as Aimee returned to the family room.

"He is," she agreed. "He's active in his church, and he has a good counseling practice. Also, he's involved in civic affairs."

"I can't imagine how a man like that has escaped being married. Or is he divorced?" Martha continued. Aimee was conscious that Samantha listened intently to the conversation.

Perhaps hoping to spare Aimee from getting too involved, Erica said, "He's never married." But she apparently couldn't resist teasing Aimee, for she slanted a look in her direction. "But maybe that's because he hasn't found the right woman before."

Aimee frowned at her and changed the conversation. "This dinner was really a nice surprise. I feel pampered tonight. It's worth turning a year older to receive so much attention. I liked *all* of my gifts."

Ed bent his long frame from the chair he'd been

sitting in. "It's time to head home, Martha. It's my turn to open the church tomorrow and check the heating system."

"Take some of the cake with you," Aimee said. "There's more left than Samantha and I can eat."

"I will," Aimee's mother said, "but don't think this conversation is finished. I expect to hear all about Jacob when you call me this week."

The time passed more quickly than Jacob had anticipated, and when he woke up on the day his grandparents were arriving, he was as excited as a kid on Christmas morning.

Since they'd chosen a Saturday, Jacob didn't have to make any changes in his counseling schedule. Gran had insisted that he invite the Mallorys to her home.

"I'll have food prepared, and if they should be here at mealtime, I can serve something without any trouble."

When Jacob talked to Aimee the night before his grandparents came, she asked, "How do you feel about it?"

"It's hard to say. I've found it difficult to forgive my father because he deserted my mother and me. Because Mother wouldn't tell me why he left, I imagined all kinds of reasons why he didn't want me."

"At least you'll have some of the mystery solved after tomorrow," Aimee assured him.

"I hope so," he answered slowly. "I only pray that what I hear will bring closure to a lot of my frustrations. It hasn't been pleasant going through life with this mystery hanging over me."

"I'll be praying for you," Aimee said.

"I'll count on that."

Soon after he hung up from talking to Aimee, the phone rang again, and it was Andrew Mallory.

"Judging from where we are now," Mr. Mallory said, "we should arrive in Benton around one o'clock tomorrow. Will that be a convenient time for you?"

"Yes, I'll be on the lookout for you."

Because he knew that Mr. Mallory had GPS in his car, Jacob gave them the street address, adding, "I live in an apartment above Gran's garage. Since she wants to meet you, too, we can visit in her living room. And she has lunch prepared for us."

Mallory thanked him and said he was looking forward to seeing him. But Jacob couldn't detect any warmth in his voice, and he wondered again just *why* they were coming. If they weren't convinced that he was their grandson, would they have bothered?

He dialed Gran's number. "I just had *the* call.

They will be here at one o'clock tomorrow. I couldn't tell by his voice whether this is a duty call or if he really wants to meet me. After all these years, I can't imagine why they started looking for me."

"This time tomorrow, we'll know," Gran said. "Try to rest."

The next morning after Jacob showered and dressed for the day, out of habit he picked up the Bible from the nightstand. He knew that his unforgiving attitude toward his father and Megan had hindered his spiritual growth for years. Every Sunday in worship service, at the end of the pastoral prayer, he had joined the congregation in praying the prayer Jesus had taught His disciples.

Over and over, he had mouthed the words *And forgive us our debts, as we forgive our debtors,* knowing that he hadn't forgiven others. He would see his assumed paternal grandparents soon, and in a few weeks he might see Megan. Wasn't it time to deal with his failure to forgive? When he learned why his father had abandoned him, the reason might be even worse than he'd imagined. Perhaps so bad, he wouldn't want to forgive. He couldn't wait until he knew the reason his father had rejected him before he dealt with his own attitude.

Jacob knelt by his chair, his head in his hands.

"Father," he prayed in a tearful voice, *"I've been miserable for years. As of now, I'm giving up the anger, the humiliation and sorrow of what my father and Megan did to me. I forgive them just as You've forgiven me of my sins."*

As he prayed, Jacob felt the cleansing wave of the Spirit touching his heart and life, wiping away the misery of the past and opening a bright and shining door to the future. Either good or bad, he was committed to the future, not to the past. Without any dread, he left the apartment and went downstairs, eager to learn what the Mallorys had to tell him.

Chapter Fifteen

Too excited to do anything constructive, he went to Gran's home, paced the floor and finally sat by a window that faced the street and waited. When a four-door sedan with two passengers pulled up alongside the curb, he uttered a silent prayer for direction. Getting up from the chair, he called, "They're here, Gran."

He breathed rapidly as he opened the front door and hurried down the walk. A white-haired heavyset man, probably in his seventies, stepped out on the sidewalk, rounded the car and opened the passenger door. A tall woman got out of the car. Her straight hair must have been blond at one time, but now it was gray and fell to her shoulders.

When Jacob reached the car, the woman walked close to him and silently scanned his face. Her eyes misted over. She threw her arms around Jacob and sobbed.

Whatever Jacob had expected, he hadn't thought he would be greeted like this. His startled eyes met those of the man who must be his grandfather.

"I'm Andrew Mallory, and this is my wife, Elizabeth." He took his wife's arm and eased her away from Jacob. "It's all right, dear," he said kindly.

"Welcome to Benton. Won't you come in, please," Jacob added in a shaky voice.

Mr. Mallory took a briefcase from the back seat and locked the car. "This is a fine home," he said.

"We think so. My grandparents..." He stumbled over the words. It seemed strange that this couple might also be his grandparents. "My maternal grandparents moved into this house when they were married, so it's been in the family for a long time."

He opened the door and motioned for the Mallorys to enter. Gran stood in the hallway. "Gran, this is Andrew and Elizabeth Mallory. My grandmother, Stella Milton. I've lived with her as long as I can remember."

Stella shook hands with them. "Welcome to our home," she said. "Jacob, take their wraps, please." Mr. Mallory took the coat from his wife's shoulders and handed it to Jacob. "I'll keep my jacket."

Gran walked ahead of them down the hall and

motioned to the living room. "This used to be the parlor in the old days," she said in her gentle voice. "And we still entertain special guests here."

Mrs. Mallory continued to weep quietly, dabbing at her eyes with a tissue. Both she and her husband seemed edgy, and Jacob sensed that they shared his fears about this meeting.

Gran seated the Mallorys on the couch, and she and Jacob sat in wingback chairs facing them. An uneasy silence filled the room, and Jacob didn't know what to say.

"Did you have a pleasant trip from Florida?" Gran asked.

"Yes," Mr. Mallory said. He fidgeted in his chair and cleared his throat. "I know this visit is difficult for you, too, and I hardly know where to start. But we might as well get on with our reason for visiting you."

He opened his briefcase and took out a framed picture and wordlessly handed it to Jacob. He stared at the portrait of a young man in an air force uniform, whose face could have been his own. The same high forehead, firm nose and chin, even a slight dimple at the corner of his mouth, which was evident on Jacob's own face when he smiled broadly.

"Now that you've seen this picture," Mrs. Mallory said, "I believe you'll forgive me for my outburst when I first saw you. I could have been looking into the face of our Philip when he was your age."

Jacob passed the photo to Gran, and she nodded. "This is your father, Jacob. I didn't see him in uniform, but I've always thought you resembled him more than you did our family."

"Even after all the information seemed to check out that you were our grandson," Mr. Mallory said, "we still couldn't keep from doubting. But one look at you convinced me. You understand that we had to be careful."

"Yes, of course, I guess," Jacob answered.

Again there was a short pause until Jacob asked quietly, "You indicated that my father is no longer living, but do you know why he abandoned me?"

The pain of his rejection must have been evident in Jacob's voice, for Mr. Mallory said, "I'm sorry, but I don't know. Our son didn't confide in us. We didn't know he had married and had a son until a few months ago."

The words seemed to be wrung out of Mrs. Mallory's heart as she whispered, "He's been dead for over thirty years." When she started crying again, her husband took her hand and held it tightly.

"We had high hopes that Philip would follow in my footsteps and enter the medical profession," Mallory explained, "and we were disappointed when he left college in his senior year and joined the air force." Looking toward Gran, he asked, "Do you know why they separated?"

She shook her head. "I met Philip only once and that was when my daughter was pregnant. They seemed quite happy, but a few months after Jacob was born, she came home to live and her lips were sealed as to why she'd left her husband. As far as I know, she never heard from him again."

"My mother died when I was six," Jacob said, and the pain in his heart must have been revealed by his words, for Stella lay her hand on his arm. "Gran raised me. I tried to get Mother to talk about my father, but she wouldn't."

"Philip was in the air force for two years, and during that time we saw him a few times," Mr. Mallory explained. "He was injured in a plane crash during a training mission. Two days later he died and his body was sent home to New York, where he's buried in a family cemetery. Since we didn't know about his marriage, naturally, we didn't search for your mother or you. He had listed "my estate" on the beneficiary line of his military insurance, so that came to us as next of kin."

Mrs. Mallory lifted her head. "That's why we didn't look for you or your mother."

"But how did you locate me now?" Jacob asked, puzzled. "When I decided to try and find out about my ancestry, I found your names in my mother's papers. But you had nothing to go on."

"We *did* when we started searching. When he was in the hospital, Philip wrote us this letter." Mallory took an envelope from his briefcase and gave it to Jacob. His hand trembled when he took the envelope.

God help me, Jacob prayed silently as he unfolded the sheet of paper, scanned it and cleared his throat. The writing was blurred and the lines were uneven, as if the writer's hands were weak.

Looking at his grandfather, Jacob said, "Is it all right if I read it aloud so Gran can hear?"

"Certainly."

After clearing his throat twice, Jacob read, "'Dear Mom and Dad, I have a serious injury, and the doctors don't give much hope for my recovery. I'm sure you've been notified by now. But there's something I must tell you—something I should have told you long ago. Three years ago, I married Marybeth Milton, a student at the university where I was enrolled. Marybeth had promised her parents she wouldn't marry until she finished college, but we were in love and we got married. Because both of us were away from our families, we thought our secret was safe until after she graduated.'"

Jacob's voice broke, and he lowered his head.

He had always wanted to know about his father, and now that he realized that his father hadn't forgotten him, his loss seemed unbearable. He cleared his throat, and resumed reading. "'Even when Marybeth got pregnant right away, we tried to keep our secret, but when her father died, I went home with her for the funeral. When her mother realized that Marybeth was pregnant, we admitted to her that we were married.'"

The writing became increasingly harder for Jacob to read, as if his father's hands were growing steadily weaker as he wrote. Or was it the mist in his eyes that blurred his vision as he continued reading?

"'The pressures of a secret marriage, the birth and care of a newborn and trying to keep up our studies made us irritable. Marybeth and I started quarreling, and after one really bad quarrel, she went home to her mother and took our son with her. I was stubborn and decided that she would have to take the first steps at reconciliation. But Marybeth was stubborn, too, and when I didn't hear from her, I quit school and enlisted.

"'Somewhere you have a grandson, Jacob Dean Mallory. Will you try to find him and see if he or his mother needs any help? I'm not proud of shirking my duty as a father and then passing my responsibilities on to you, but I thought I would have time to...'"

The letter ended abruptly and Jacob envisioned that scene in the hospital when his father's hand was no longer able to hold the pen. Had he died then, or…? Tears blurred his eyes and he handed the letter back to his grandfather. Gran knelt by Jacob's chair, and she took his hand and clasped it tightly.

"So now you know at last," she said. "It's a bittersweet moment to gain a father and lose him in the same day, but he did love you and his last thoughts were of you."

Mr. Mallory cleared his throat and said huskily, "Yes, he wanted us to see if you needed anything. I'm only sorry we are so late in finding you."

Looking around the room, Mrs. Mallory said, "It's obvious that you've not been in need. This must have been a great home environment for you."

"Yes, Gran has been wonderful to me, but I've always missed not having a father, especially when I wondered why he didn't want me."

"But there's something I don't understand," Gran said. "Philip died over thirty years ago, yet you say that you haven't known about Jacob very long."

In a strained voice, Mr. Mallory explained. "A few months ago we received a small packet in the mail. It seems that the army hospital in Germany where Philip died was recently renovating its oldest wing. While tearing out some cabinets in the mailroom, they came across a bag of mail that had been covered with boxes of old medical records. Philip's letter was in that bag, and it was forwarded to us. That's when we started searching for you."

Silence wrapped the room like a shroud, until his grandfather asked Jacob, "You've never married?"

"No," Jacob answered.

"We had hoped that we might not find not only a grandson, but also some more grandchildren," Mrs. Mallory said.

"Then you have other children besides my father?"

"Yes, two daughters and five grandchildren. They live in New York, and we miss them during our visits to Florida," Mrs. Mallory said. "We're eager to get home to see them, and that's the reason for our short visit. And, of course," she added, "we didn't know what to expect here."

"We must be on our way soon," Mr. Mallory said, "but there are a few business matters that I need to discuss with you."

He took some papers out of his briefcase. "We have never spent the insurance money Philip left. We invested it, and it's grown to a tidy sum through the years. It's yours as soon as we can take care of the legal transfer."

"That's generous of you, but it isn't necessary," Jacob objected. He explained about his counseling business. "I make a good living, so please keep the money you received from my father. I don't want it."

When Mallory started to protest, Jacob added, "You've already given me a priceless gift. You've given me a father—something I've always wanted. After a lifetime of believing that my father didn't want me, to learn that he acknowledged me on his deathbed is a gift that money can't buy. And to know that you're willing to accept me into the family means more to me than money."

"Nevertheless, the money is yours," his grandfather insisted, "and I'm going to transfer it to your name as soon as I talk with my accountant. I will need your social security number and other pertinent information. You can leave it in the same investment firm if you like, but the money is yours."

Jacob was too overwhelmed to answer. He looked at Gran to see her reaction to all they had heard. She shook her head, indicating that she wouldn't advise him about accepting the insurance money.

"I mentioned that I have a counseling business," he said, "but I didn't mention Substitute Siblings, an organization that Gran and I established to help children in need. Perhaps I can use part of the money to support new projects there."

"The money is yours to do with as you like,"

Mallory said. "I'll have it transferred as soon as possible."

After he recorded the information he needed, Jacob answered all their questions about his growing-up years and his education. And he was interested to hear about the two aunts he had in New York and also about his father's childhood.

Three hours later when Gran and Jacob stood on the sidewalk watching the Mallorys drive away, Jacob still wondered if he was awake or if he'd dreamed the afternoon's events. When his grand-parents' car turned the corner, Gran and Jacob exchanged glances. She grinned delightedly at him.

"I've prayed for this day for years," she said.

"It's a red-letter day, all right. Not only did I inherit grandparents, two aunts and several cousins, but also Substitute Siblings will have some additional funds to help more kids."

"I'm glad you agreed to visit them this fall," Gran said.

"They invited you, too," Jacob reminded her. "You must go with me."

"But I won't. That experience will be for you and your father's family. I've had you all of your life—it's their turn. I won't intrude."

Jacob really didn't want to go alone, and if Gran wouldn't go with him, he wished that Aimee would, but there was only one way that was possible. Now that the mystery of his heritage had been cleared up, he was free to deepen his relationship with Aimee, but was he ready to acquire a stepdaughter? He knew if he married Aimee, Samantha was part of the package, too.

He could have called Aimee, but somehow he wanted to be with her, see the expression on her face when he told her about his grandparents' visit. She had planned an outing with Chloe, and he waited until he was sure she'd be home by the time he drove to her house. She came to the door when he rang the bell.

"Oh, come in," she said. "I've thought about you all day wondering how the visit with your grandparents went."

"It couldn't have been better. Do you have time to hear about it?"

"Sure! I can't wait to find out."

They sat side by side on the couch in the living room, while Jacob told her the details of the visit, even the amount of the insurance money he would eventually receive.

"My grandparents live in Malone, New York, and I have two aunts and some cousins who live there, too. They had a family picture, and it seems that they're all God-fearing people who would be a credit to any family tree."

"So you see, you've been worrying needlessly,"

she said and pushed back the hair that had fallen over his forehead.

"Yes, but wouldn't you have worried, too, if you were in my situation?"

"Of course I would. Are you going to visit them?"

"Yes, in the fall. At least, before my grandparents go to Florida again for the winter."

She leaned against him, and Jacob put his arm around her shoulders. "You can't imagine what a burden has been lifted from my shoulders."

"Yes, I can…I can tell by the absence of a hint of sadness that always seemed to be lurking in your eyes. I pray that I'll never see it there again."

Jacob took her face and held it gently, kissed her and cradled her in his arms. She returned his caresses eagerly, until at last they were content to just sit in a close embrace and savor their moments together. Jacob looked ahead, praying that their future years would be as poignant as this moment they shared.

He went home jubilant, feeling that his problems were behind him. His paternal grandparents had recognized him and wanted to become a part of his life. Samantha was becoming less antagonistic about his relationship with Aimee. Everything was falling into place for Aimee and him to plan a life together. He couldn't envision a cloud in the sky of their future happiness.

* * *

The next afternoon when the phone rang, not only did a cloud hover on the horizon, Jacob knew immediately that he faced a storm of gigantic proportions.

"Jacob," said a voice he hadn't heard for years, "this is Megan Russell."

He was momentarily speechless in his surprise, and his body stiffened in shock.

"Jacob?" Megan said again.

"Yes," he managed to squeeze out the one word from a throat that seemed temporarily numbed by disbelief.

"I'm coming to Benton for the big celebration next month, and I'd like to see you. I owe you an apology and an explanation of what happened between us. I wouldn't blame you if you refused to see me, but it's time I set the record straight."

She spoke calmly, seemingly unaware that she had pulled an emotional rug from under his feet.

Jacob had believed he had forgiven Megan for the trouble and anguish she had caused him, but when he heard her voice, all of the anger he'd once harbored against her surfaced. When he spoke, his voice was quiet, although he knew it carried an undertone of his resentment.

"I can't believe it. After shaming me before the whole town of Benton and allowing people to think I'd fathered your child, you have the audacity to believe that a mere apology can set things right between us?"

Jacob pictured Megan shrugging her shoulders before she answered, "Well, it's up to you. Do you think you're the only one who's been miserable? I cared about you, Jacob, and I'm not proud of what I did. I had to make a choice between embarrassing you and naming the father of my child. I am sorry I treated you the way I did, but frankly I thought you could deal with the disgrace easier than he could. As I said, I care for you, but I loved him."

Jacob thought her comments were too bizarre to deserve an answer. "No, I don't want to see you, Megan. By the mercy of God, I've forgiven you for the way you treated me, and I'll accept your apology. I've lived down the bad reputation you foisted upon me. So, let's leave it at that. I don't want to see you, and I prefer that you stay away from Benton. If you come back, all the gossip of the past will be resurrected. I don't think I deserve that."

"I *am* coming to Benton for the celebration. I'll try to sneak in and out of town without making any waves, but I still think we should talk. I owe you an explanation, but it's up to you. I'll call after I get to Benton, in case you change your mind."

She hung up, and almost immediately, Jacob wished he had learned more. Where did she live? He checked quickly to see if his caller ID had registered her telephone number. It hadn't. Jacob buried his head in his hands.

"God, why? Why did she have to return now? It took years to get over the rejection I had from Megan and from my friends and neighbors who believed I was guilty. Why did she have to return after I've found Aimee and want to spend my future with her? Why, God?"

Chapter Sixteen

Jacob was busy with the celebration, especially the dedication of the memorial plaque for David Harwood, and he didn't contact Aimee for several days leading up to the celebration. She was relieved, for now that Jacob's heritage was no longer a secret. She was convinced that he loved her, but worried about Samantha. Would he want to marry her in light of Samantha's coolness? Except for asking Jacob to the birthday dinner—and Aimee suspected that Erica had twisted her arm to get that to happen—Samantha never mentioned Jacob to her. Aimee agonized over what answer she could give if Jacob asked her to marry him.

Jennifer's injuries were serious enough that she had to be homeschooled, but by the end of June, she was released by her doctor. Driving her mother's car, she came to see Samantha. Aimee hardly knew her when she walked in the door.

Jennifer anticipated Aimee's surprise, and being Jennifer, she didn't hesitate to comment on it. She spread her arms wide and pirouetted for Aimee and Samantha. Her hair was cut in a light brown, short bob. She had on one set of earrings only, a pair of navy blue capris and a white knit blouse.

"Whoo-hoo! The new me!" Mimicking her father, she said, "'As long as you live under my roof, young lady, you're going to dress like any other red-blooded American girl rather than some monster from outer space.'"

Aimee couldn't hold back her laughter.

"I don't believe this!" Samantha said.

"Which means my Gothic look is gone. No black clothing, no chains *and* only one pair of earrings." With lifted eyebrows, she said, her eyes twinkling, "In fact, my father made me take a solemn oath to never again wear a black garment in his presence. And that includes not wearing black to his funeral."

Samantha was laughing so hard, she held her sides.

"Okay, enough!" she cried.

Jennifer joined Aimee and Samantha in laughing. "Oh, well, I kinda like the simple style. I was trying to make a statement with my Gothic appearance. And my mom has had her share of criticism for not watching me more closely. She's determined to do what Dad says. I'll walk the straight and narrow through the rest of high school. If I don't, Dad will make me attend college in Richmond where he can keep his eye on me. I want to go to Harvard."

"How you'd get here, Jen?"

"I've got Mother's car, but only to drive over here."

"Are you going to the celebration tomorrow?" Samantha asked.

"Oh, but yes! Dad is going to make a speech," Jennifer said, rolling her eyes. "Our whole family will be there."

"I wish we could sit together," Samantha said with a disappointed look.

"Dad has some reserved seats with a bunch of big shots. But if I can, I'll sneak away and sit with you."

While Jennifer and Samantha were hanging out in her room, the phone rang.

"Aimee, this is Allie Slater. I think the festivities will be too much for me tomorrow, but Chloe wants to go. Would it be too much trouble for you to stop by and pick her up?"

"Not at all. We'll plan to get there in time for the picnic at noon and stay through the two-hour program that ends at four."

When she hung up, Aimee realized that she was

maturing as much as she hoped Samantha was. A few weeks ago, she would probably have asked Samantha if it was all right to take Chloe. It was no wonder that Samantha had thought she called all the shots in the house. Aimee had allowed her to think so.

In a half hour, Samantha and Jennifer came upstairs. "I've got to leave," Jennifer said. "Still on probation, you know. Dad's really surprised me. He's laid down ultimatums before but he always forgot them after a day or two. He won't back down this time. Don't tell anyone, but I'm finding the more structured life kinda cool."

"Who called, Mom?"

"Mrs. Slater. She wants us to stop by and take Chloe to the celebration tomorrow."

Samantha flashed a quick look toward Jennifer. "I've been hanging out with Chloe a little."

"Yeah, Madison told me. Madison says she's all right."

"Kinda shy, but she's a cool kid," Samantha said. "You'll like her."

"Bound to," Jennifer agreed. Again, imitating her father's deep voice, she said, "'It's time you made more friends. If you broaden your vision, you'll find out that a lot of the students at that school are worth knowing, instead of just a handful.'"

Aimee grinned as she called goodbye to

Jennifer as Samantha walked out to the car with her. Mr. Nibert might have forced his daughter into a more disciplined life, but he certainly hadn't broken her spirit.

When Samantha came back in, Aimee said, "It's good to have Jennifer back again."

"It's awesome. All of us have grown up a little, though. Maybe the car wreck wasn't so bad, after all."

"Thanks for being nice to Chloe."

"She's all right, but I still like Madison and Jen best."

"That's understandable. I didn't expect you to take Chloe as your best friend. I just don't want you to mistreat her. She needs help, and helping her has been good for me."

"I've never mistreated her," Samantha protested.

Knowing that a few months ago her daughter would have resented Chloe, Aimee said, "No, you haven't, and I appreciate that. I know you never wanted me to work with the Sibling organization. I can't understand why exactly. I've never neglected you."

Aimee didn't look at Samantha, but she heard her scuffing her shoes on the tiled floor. "I guess I was afraid. It's not so much that I don't want you to help Chloe, but poor kids scare me. I'm afraid I might end up like them sometime. If anything happens to you, I wouldn't have anyone to take care of me. It's not easy being the child of a single mother and no father."

"Samantha, you should have told me sooner," Aimee said, shocked and almost in tears. "It's not likely that anything is going to happen to me, and if it did, Dad and Mom would have welcomed you to their home in a heartbeat. And Grandmother Blake would have been there for you. You would have been well taken care of."

"But still no dad," Samantha whispered.

Aimee's heart thudded. "But I've always thought you wouldn't want me to get married again. That's one reason I haven't dated before. Wouldn't you resent a stepfather?"

"Depends on who it is, I guess. Some guys aren't so bad."

"It might have been better if we'd had this talk years ago," Aimee said with a sigh. But she knew she wouldn't have wanted anyone for a husband except Jacob. Maybe Samantha was hinting that her relationship with him wasn't so bad. But since she couldn't yet promise Samantha any future with Jacob, she ignored the insinuation in Samantha's comment.

Although Jacob had once looked forward to the bicentennial celebration, all he wanted now was to get it over with and know that Megan Russell had left town. When she had called again last night, he'd finally agreed to meet her in Pioneer Park as soon as the dedication ceremony was over.

When he reached the courthouse square, Jacob made his way to the platform. He saw Aimee and the girls and waved to them. Shortly after the festivities opened with the singing of the national anthem and a speech by the mayor, Jacob took his seat among the planning committee members and others who would participate in the program.

Jacob found it difficult to focus on the various presentations. His thoughts kept drifting to his upcoming meeting with Megan. He wished now that he'd told Aimee about her call, or that he had refused to see Megan. Time seemed to crawl until he finally stood and walked to the podium.

A hint of expectancy settled over the audience and Jacob lost some of his stage fright. "At this time," he said, "I'll ask Andrea Horton, wife of David, and their two children to come forward and unveil the plaque, which will be subsequently placed on the Wall of Honor in the office of the local board of education."

A well-dressed, somber-eyed woman, seated on the front row, stood and motioned for her children to precede her to the platform. Although the Harwoods had lived in Benton for years, he didn't remember seeing Mrs. Harwood before. Jacob had heard that she was somewhat reclusive, a sharp contrast to her husband who was always in the public eye.

The two children appeared to be in their teens. The daughter bore a remarkable resemblance to the photograph of Dr. Harwood, which had been placed under a glass shield in the center of the plaque.

Smiling with an effort, Jacob presented his speech, ending with, "It's my pleasure, on behalf of the city of Benton, to honor David Harwood today as an educational and civic leader of this city for many years. His death left a void in the leadership of our city. However, our city is proud of his legacy."

Jacob handed Mrs. Harwood a remote that would pull the curtain from the front of the plaque. The curtain rolled back to reveal the bronze memorial, and he read the inscription on the plaque.

When he finished, Jacob handed Mrs. Harwood the microphone. She hesitated briefly before she took it, and seemingly speaking with an effort, she said, "My children and I are thankful for the honor you have paid David today. He was very fond of the people of Benton."

Jacob shook hands with her and her children and walked with them off the platform. As

Jacob's eyes followed her and the children to their seats, he was stunned to see Megan Russell sitting directly behind the Harwood family.

Although he hadn't seen her for almost twenty years, he knew it was Megan. He turned away, hoping he had shown no sign of recognition.

Two hours later Jacob reluctantly drove into Pioneer Park where he'd arranged to meet Megan. He felt that he was being disloyal to Aimee to come here at all and certainly without telling her that Megan had returned.

A red SUV was parked near the fountain, and when he pulled into the parking lot, Megan stepped out of it. The years had not been kind to her. She was overweight, and the heavy makeup she wore did little to conceal the lines around her eyes and forehead—wrinkles too deeply etched for someone her age. Her expression was tight with strain, and Jacob wondered if she was also uneasy about their meeting.

Looking around the park, she asked, "Can we go someplace and have dinner? This is pretty public."

Jacob shook his head. Uncompromisingly, he said, "Not as public as a restaurant, and I don't want to be seen with you. I've worked hard to rebuild my reputation in Benton, and I probably shouldn't have met you at all. But I've never completely let go of the past, and I don't think I ever will without learning why you ruined my reputation without a word to set the record straight."

"You've never married?" Megan said, and her eyes searched his face, as if she was trying to read his thoughts.

"Not yet," he answered shortly.

"Does that mean that you're planning to be married?"

"We didn't come here to discuss my marital plans," Jacob said coldly. "What do you have to tell me?"

For a long moment Megan looked at him, and Jacob grew uncomfortable under her gaze, before she said, "If it will make you feel any better, I've always felt mean that I let people think you were the father of my daughter."

"So the baby was a girl?" he asked. "Where is she, by the way? How has her life been?"

"She's with my parents this weekend. They've been very supportive. Karen and I live with them. I couldn't have made it on my own."

Apparently the father of the child had given no support to Megan and the little girl. Jacob looked at his watch. "I can't stay long," he reminded her.

She took a colored photo from her pocket. "This is my daughter. David Harwood was the father of my child."

Jacob was speechless in his surprise, but he

didn't doubt her word. The girl looked just like Harwood. Bile rose in his throat, when he thought of the town's efforts to honor a man who had not only fathered a child out of wedlock, but also let another man be blamed for what he had done.

He didn't doubt that Megan was telling the truth, and suddenly incidents in the past surged forward in his mind—things that made more sense to him now. Why Megan had suddenly taken an interest in after-school activities. Why she seemed happy one day but stressed out and bitter the next.

"Can't you understand now why I couldn't tell?" Megan asked in a pleading voice. "Think of all the things he's accomplished in this town. None of that would have happened if people had known. He was already married when he came to Benton, but we fell in love. His wife was pregnant, and when I got pregnant, too, I tried to seduce you so you'd think it was your child. I loved David too much to ruin his life."

"But you didn't care if you ruined mine," Jacob said bitterly.

Much of the despair that Jacob had experienced years ago resurfaced. The humiliation, the degradation, the sense of rejection he'd known then rushed back as if he was eighteen again. He felt unclean even to be in Megan's presence, and he wished he had never heard this sordid revelation.

He turned his back on his high-school girlfriend, walked to his car, settled wearily into the seat and drove away. He felt emotionally and physically ill. For years he had condemned himself for not marrying Megan and giving the child a name. Now to realize that she had attempted to seduce him because she needed a scapegoat to protect David Harwood opened the old wounds Jacob thought he'd put behind him.

He had only driven for a few yards when he stopped and backed his car to where Megan stood. He got out of the car and took her hand.

"I shouldn't have been so harsh with you, Megan. I know now what it's like to really love someone. I'd go to any length to protect her, so I understand why you tried to use me. Perhaps I should have done more to help you, but I was young, too, and terribly hurt." He squeezed her hand and released it. "I forgive you, Megan, as I pray God will forgive me for my harsh thoughts about you."

He got into the car, took one last look at her tear-streaked face and headed toward Benton.

Chapter Seventeen

Aimee was seated far back in the crowd, and she didn't make eye contact with Jacob during the whole program. He had waved before he took his seat at the rear of the platform where she couldn't see him.

She'd kept putting him off when he wanted to talk about the future, but now in spite of anything, even Samantha's objections, she would marry him if he asked her. She knew she loved him, and that he was the right man for her.

Jennifer apparently hadn't been able to slip away from her father's group, but after the ceremony, she joined them.

"Mrs. Blake, it sure would be nice if you'd let Sam come for a sleepover tonight," she said. "Dad is still calling the shots at home. I'm grounded from going out. I don't blame my parents. I was getting too wild, but I'm just plain bored."

Aimee had noted an absence of the flippant, adult-like air that Jennifer had been exhibiting for a year or more. She believed that during her convalescence, the girl had come to terms with her behavior.

"I won't agree until I talk to your parents. Now that school is out, I'm willing to ease up on the restrictions. I'll call from my cell when we get to the car."

"They'll say it's okay," Jennifer said confidently. With a cute grin, she added, "Riding herd on me is getting to be a bore." She looked at Chloe, who had seemed quieter than usual, perhaps awed by Jennifer's dominating personality. "You might as well come, too, Chloe. Madison is away this weekend."

Chloe's face turned red, and she stammered, "I'd like to, but I don't know what Grandma will say."

"Let's see if Jennifer's parents agree, and then I'll check with your grandmother," Aimee suggested, secretly pleased that Chloe was being included.

Aimee spent the next two hours confirming with Mr. Nibert that Jennifer could have a sleepover, getting permission from Mrs. Slater for Chloe to go, stopping by Chloe's home for overnight clothes, going to her own home for Samantha to pack and then delivering all three girls to the Nibert home.

It was seven o'clock when she finally semicollapsed in the lounge chair, disappointed that there wasn't a message from Jacob. He hadn't been calling as often as he had, and she made herself believe that it was because he was too busy with the bicentennial. But his responsibilities were behind him now, and she hoped he would contact her. When he hadn't called by eleven, she went to bed. She was still awake when the phone rang an hour later. Startled and fearful, she picked up the phone.

"Aimee, this is Stella Milton. I hope I didn't wake you up."

"No, I'm in bed, but I haven't gone to sleep. My mind is still full of today's activities to rest."

"It was a nice day, but I didn't call to talk about that. Jacob hasn't come home, and I'm worried about him. I thought you might know where he is."

Aimee chose her words carefully, for she didn't want Stella to know that they weren't seeing each other much. "I haven't talked with him today," she said, "and I don't know where he is."

"I guess I'm a worrisome old woman, and I don't often check on Jacob's whereabouts, but I had a message from his grandfather, and I wanted to pass it along. I've tried his cell phone and the phone in his apartment. I suppose I wouldn't be worried if I hadn't noticed that he's been preoccupied the past few days, as if he's worried about something. I haven't seen him like this since he was a boy."

"Have you tried the office? He might have gone there after the ceremony," Aimee suggested.

"I didn't call the office because the switchboard would be off," Stella said. "I contacted the security guard at the complex. He said that Jacob came there this evening, but he didn't see him leave. I'm worried."

Throwing back the covers, Aimee said, "Samantha is at a sleepover, so I'll go check on him. He loaned me a key to the office a few weeks ago so I could borrow some counseling videos he had received. I haven't returned it."

"I probably should go with you," Stella said.

"No, that isn't necessary," Aimee assured her. "I'll call you as soon as I find him. Don't worry. I'm sure he's catching up on work he's missed the past couple of weeks."

As she quickly dressed in a pair of jeans and a sweatshirt, Aimee wished she was as confident as she pretended to be. Fearful pictures of what she might find at Jacob's office flitted through her mind. To calm her nerves, when she was dressed, she knelt beside her chair, and with her hand on the Bible, prayed for God to guide her.

Because Saturday-night traffic wasn't heavy in the section of Benton where Jacob's office was located, Aimee arrived at the security gate more rapidly than she anticipated. She punched in the entrance code, waved to the guard and drove to the parking lot in front of the building. She didn't know whether to be relieved or alarmed that Jacob's car was still parked in the lot. Light shone from his office window.

She inserted her key card into the slot, punched in the code, opened the door and walked quickly upstairs. The door to Jacob's office stood open, and catching her breath, she hurried inside. Jacob was slumped over his desk, his hands outstretched. She stifled a scream.

"Jacob," she said, and he didn't stir.

She rushed to the desk, searched for and found a steady pulse in his neck. "Thank God," she breathed. She shook his shoulder until he stirred.

"Jacob," she said loudly.

He raised his head and stared at her. He shook his head as if to clear his vision. "What's going on? Why are you here?"

She laughed in relief. "Well, you've almost scared Stella and me to death. It's after midnight. Are you sick?"

"Yeah, sick," he said, "but not the kind of sick you mean. My spirit is sick. I had a few things I needed to do, and I've been here since eight o'clock. I took some medication for a splitting headache, laid my head on the desk and that's the last I remember. I'm not used to taking pain medication, and it put me out. I left my cell in the car."

Aimee took her cell phone from her purse. "I'll call Stella and tell her you're all right."

While Aimee talked to Stella to put her mind at ease, Jacob walked around the room, swinging his arms. He dropped to the floor and executed several push-ups.

"I'll go wash my face and meet you in the snack room. I think I'm awake enough to drive home, but I'd better drink a cup of coffee or a soda."

"Which do you prefer? I'll fix it for you."

"Make it a Coke. And fix something for yourself."

Now that Stella knew that Jacob was all right, and since her cell phone was on if Samantha should need her, Aimee decided there was no better time or place to find out where she stood with Jacob. He came into the snack room while she was pouring the drink over the ice cubes.

They sat on opposite sides of one of the tables. "I'm glad you came, Aimee. The reason I didn't go home was because I need to tell you something, which I should have told you before this."

"I'm aware that there's something wrong between us," she said. "What have I done to push you away?"

"You haven't done anything." He took a deep breath and closed his eyes, apparently reluctant to speak. "A few weeks ago I had a call from

Megan Russell, telling me that she was coming to the bicentennial and wanted to see me."

His voice was absolutely emotionless, and Aimee felt momentary panic as her mind jumped forward.

"At first," he said, "I refused to see her, but when she called again last night, I went to meet her in Pioneer Park after the celebration."

Feeling as if the breath had been knocked out of her, Aimee whispered, "Why didn't you tell me?"

"I didn't know what to do," Jacob said, and his voice sounded tired. "I kept hoping she wouldn't show up, and I've been almost desperate wondering if her presence in town would stir up that old scandal again. When I met her today, she indicated that she had only arranged to meet me to apologize for the way she'd treated me."

A tense silence surrounded them, and Aimee clenched her hands until the nails pierced her skin.

Jacob's voice drifted into a hoarse whisper. "She told me some things that shocked me so much that I don't know if I should ever repeat them. However, our interview had one important outcome. I'd always wondered if I should have protected her name and married her anyway. After what I heard today, I'll never think that again."

Aimee sensed that what Megan had told Jacob had hurt him terribly, and she didn't want to add to his pain. "You don't have to tell me anything. What happened between you and Megan is in the past, the same as my marriage to Steve is behind me. I love you, Jacob, love you for what you are now. You've become a fine man in spite of that unfortunate experience."

Jacob lunged out of his chair as if he'd been stung by a hornet. His weariness seemed to have disappeared as he pulled her upward, and Aimee knew she'd said the right words to bring him around.

Jacob snuggled Aimee close for a few precious moments before he held her at arm's length. "I love you, too, and I've wanted to tell you so for weeks, but there never seemed to be a right time. Does this mean you'll marry me?"

"Yes. That is, if you want to take on me and my teenager."

Aimee's feet seemed to be drifting on cloud nine and happiness filled her heart as his hands slipped up her arms, pulling her closer. She put her arms around his neck, and she felt his lips touch hers. After a heady moment, she buried her head in his shoulder.

"Have you talked this over with Samantha?" he whispered into her hair.

She shook her head. "This is between you and me. I want Samantha to be pleased about it, and from something she said a few days ago, I think she will accept it, but whatever she says, I won't change my mind."

"I'll do everything I can to win Samantha over, but as you say, it will be the two of us." He smiled and quoted a line from the marriage service, "'And these two shall be one.' But I won't marry you with secrets. Let's go into the lounge."

Seated close together, with Aimee's head on his shoulder, Jacob told her everything he had heard from Megan about David Harwood. When he finished, he said, "If I make this public, it will hurt numerous people, but it doesn't seem right for this town to honor a man who's lived a lie for years. What is the right thing for me to do with what I've heard?"

"Do you think she's lying?"

"No. She had a picture of her daughter who could be a twin of the girl with Mrs. Harwood today."

Aimee chose her words carefully. "David Harwood is in the hands of a merciful God who will judge him. You and I can't do it. And we certainly shouldn't add any more pain to Mrs. Harwood, who has held her head up in Benton all of these years and stayed with him in spite of his infidelity."

"Then you think I shouldn't repeat it."

"No, you should not," she said confidently. "Actually, I don't think it's your secret to tell. You also need to consider the effect this would have on the residents of Benton, those who've looked up to Mr. Harwood. And on his innocent daughters. For all we know, this may have been the only mark on his character."

"That's sound advice, Aimee, and I'm going to follow it. I need to consider Mrs. Harwood and her children. If this news should be made public, they would be hurt very much."

"Exactly! Although you were hurt by all of this, you've survived the ridicule and become a respected man in Benton. It's time to move on and put the past behind you."

Jacob pulled her close into his arms. "That's exactly what I wanted to do, but I wrestled with my conscience for hours, trying to make the right decision." He kissed the tip of her nose. "So I'm moving on. Tell me when you'll marry me."

"Let's give our families a few weeks to get used to the idea and get married before fall."

Jacob's eyes brimmed with tenderness. "It can't be too soon for me."

It was time for them to leave, but Aimee was too content to break this magical moment when she knew with certainty that she and Jacob had been made for each other. They had both lived through the storms of their separate lives before they'd finally found a safe harbor in each other.

Chapter Eighteen

"Looks like a postcard scene, doesn't it?" Jacob whispered in Aimee's ear as he leaned across her to peer out the small window. The huge jet lowered its wheels and, slowly losing altitude, cruised toward Honolulu International Airport.

"Pinch me. I think I'm still dreaming," Aimee said.

Playfully, Jacob pressed her wrist between his thumb and forefinger. "I feel the same way. Everything happened so fast that I can't believe that after several months of turmoil, we're really getting married."

"And in Hawaii, too," Aimee said. "I've always thought that Hawaii would be a great place for a honeymoon, but that we're actually being married here, too, is hard to believe."

"And to think that after Samantha balked so

long at our relationship, she would be the one who suggested this."

Lowering her voice, Aimee said, "I'm still not sure she didn't just see this as a good way to get a trip to Hawaii—something that neither Jennifer nor Madison has ever done."

"Well, whatever brought it on," Jacob said, "I couldn't be happier."

As she fastened her seat belt for the landing, Aimee glanced around the cabin. Gran and Samantha sat across the aisle to their left. Seated directly behind Aimee and Jacob were her parents and Erica, and Andrew and Elizabeth Mallory were seated in front of them.

It had all started when Samantha was surfing the Net and saw advertisements about package-deal Hawaiian weddings. She had downloaded a brochure with all the details.

Aimee smiled at Jacob, and knew that he, too, was recalling the evening they were sitting in the family room watching television when Samantha had strolled in. She said, "If you two guys ever get around to getting married, you might want this."

She handed them the brochure and left as quietly as she'd walked in. They spent the rest of the evening looking over the printout until Aimee had said, "This sounds like a good idea." Jacob thought so, too, and now here they were.

"I just about backed out," Jacob said, "when I found out so many people wanted to go with us. I was looking forward to being alone with you for a few days."

"But I knew it would mean a lot to us and disappoint our loved ones if they didn't get to see us get married."

"At least we held our ground," Jacob said, "and wouldn't agree to having them go with us until they agreed to give us some time alone. They'll have to entertain themselves for three days while we're honeymooning in a secluded cottage."

While they taxied to the airport and waited for the skyway to be attached to the plane, Jacob commented, "It's amazing how quickly Gran and my other grandparents have bonded."

"And my parents fit right in, too," Aimee agreed.

"And it does mean a lot to have my father's parents with me," Jacob said with tenderness in his voice. "I still want to visit his grave, so we'll take a few days and go to New York before my grandparents return to Florida for the winter. I would have gone sooner, but I wanted you to be with me."

They filed through the crowded airport on their way to the baggage claim to the sounds of Hawaiian music. And while they were waiting for their luggage, a Hawaiian couple, carrying a large placard with Blake-Mallory on it approached them.

"Are you Jacob Mallory?" the man asked, approaching Jacob with a wide grin.

"Yes, and this is my fiancée, Aimee." The other six family members and Erica crowded close, and Jacob introduced them.

"My name is Kaio, your on-site coordinator." He put his arm around the woman beside him. "This is my wife, Nateli. She will take you to the van. Give me your luggage checks," the man said, "and I'll join you as soon as I collect your luggage."

"Come this way," Nateli said, and when they reached the van, she put a lei around each of their necks, and said, "Welcome to Hawaii."

From her window seat in the van, Aimee watched as Kaio hurried toward the bus, followed by a man with their luggage on a carrier. As soon as the luggage was stored underneath the bus, Kaio joined them in the small van. The driver closed the door and drove out of the parking lot.

"As we travel into the city, I'll give you information about the next two days," Kaio said. "For today, you can check into your hotel and have the remainder of this day and tomorrow morning free as you requested."

Aimee took a small notebook from her purse and made notes on what he was saying. "All of the arrangements have been made according to our agreement earlier. The wedding will take place on

Waikiki Beach tomorrow evening at sunset. After the ceremony and a dinner at the hotel, the bridal couple will go by limousine to a wedding cottage reserved for them on the far side of the island. We have arranged bus tours for the rest of you until they return at the end of the third day."

He mentioned that after the honeymoon, when Jacob and Aimee had rejoined them, arrangements had been made for all of them to have a three-day tour to the islands of Kauai and Maui before they returned home.

Looking directly at Jacob, Kaio said, "Is all of this satisfactory?"

"Yes, sir," Jacob assured him, smiling at his bride-to-be. "Exactly as we planned it."

Contrary to tradition that the groom wasn't to see the bride on the day of the wedding, Jacob and Aimee ate breakfast with the rest of the family. As soon as Aimee had asked Samantha to be her only attendant, Samantha had said, "That will be pretty fun, Mom. Let's buy both of our dresses after we get to Hawaii."

As soon as breakfast was over on their first morning in Hawaii, Aimee and Samantha started shopping. Since Aimee had a formal wedding dress when she married Steve, she decided to wear a Hawaiian dress this time.

After shopping for most of the morning, they found a dress that Samantha liked, a floral print that flowed gracefully to her ankles.

Pirouetting before the mirror, she said, "I like it, Mom. Let's choose something for you."

Aimee had already decided, but she wanted Samantha to choose first. "I want this dress with blue and white flowers."

"That's the one," Samantha agreed. "That blue is the same color as your eyes. What about a veil?"

"No. I don't want one. I'm going to the beauty shop in the hotel this afternoon. As part of our ceremony, I'm going to wear a yellow hibiscus in my hair. Before we're married, I'll put it over my right ear, and after the ceremony, Jacob will put it on the left side, to symbolize that we're married."

"Cool," Samantha approved.

Walking slowly along the streets, window-shopping, they made their way back to their multistoried hotel. Before they joined the others, Aimee stopped and turned Samantha to face her. Looking deeply into her daughter's eyes, Aimee said, "And you're sure you're all right with this?"

With a sneaky grin on her face, Samantha said, "And if I say no does that mean you won't go through with the wedding?"

Aimee's spirits ebbed a little at the question, but she was encouraged by Samantha's grin. She shook her head. "No, I love Jacob and I'm going to marry him, but I hope you're okay with it."

"Mom, it's all right. I like him. I'm sorry I was such a jerk before, but I've grown up a lot since then. I know it's important for you to have a life, because when I go to college, you're not coming with me." She stood on tiptoe and kissed Aimee, and with a sigh of relief, Aimee laughed and hugged her close.

Prenuptial ukulele music played by two women greeted the wedding party as they sat in the chairs provided for them in a secluded area of the beach. The setting sun shed a kaleidoscope of bright colors around them, as Aimee and Jacob stood beneath a floral bridal arch and faced Diamondhead, Honolulu's famous landmark, to take their vows.

Andrew Mallory was Jacob's attendant, and Samantha stood at Aimee's side. The woman who married them wore a traditional Hawaiian dress, and Aimee was glad that she and Samantha had chosen to dress informally, too. At the conclusion of the ceremony, the musicians played and sang "The Lord's Prayer."

Because their wedding party was small, they had dispensed with a reception, but the family gathered around them as soon as they took their vows. With a sidelong glance, Aimee noted that

Samantha accepted Jacob's embrace and kiss on the forehead.

Thank you, God, she prayed silently. *I know that Samantha and I are in safe with Jacob. But it will take a lot of guidance from You to make the three of us into a family.*

When Jacob and Aimee reached the limousine that would take them to their cottage, Aimee threw her bridal bouquet. To the delight of everyone, Erica caught it, and Jacob said, "Serves you right. It's about time we matched you up!"

Aimee wakened the next morning with her head on Jacob's shoulder. She had slept so soundly that for a moment she wondered if she was dreaming. But their wedding, the dinner and a quick trip to the wedding cottage by limousine hadn't been a dream. Before they arrived at the cottage, her old fears about the intimacies of marriage had surfaced, but this morning her worries were gone. No longer would she be concerned about being the kind of wife she wanted to be.

Through the open window, Aimee heard the constant rhythm of the incoming waves on the sandy beach. It was not yet daylight, but she slipped out of bed and went to the balcony. Through a grove of coconut trees, a quarter moon hovered over the Pacific. As daylight neared she saw whitecaps slapping on the sandy beach.

She sensed Jacob's presence behind her, and he put his arms around her and led her to the metal bench on the balcony. She leaned against his chest.

"I didn't mean to wake you," she said, "but I'm glad we can share this beautiful scene."

"Let's dress and go wade in the surf," Jacob suggested. "We have a private beach, so we won't disturb anyone else."

A short time later as they strolled along the small beach, the breeze ruffling their hair, and the cool water splashing around their feel, the large orb of the sun popped into view over a haze-filled horizon.

"Good morning, Mrs. Mallory," Jacob said. "Is it too early to tell you I love you?"

"It's never too early to hear that," Aimee answered. "In fact, I'm expecting to hear it every morning for the rest of our lives."

"And God willing," Jacob said reverently, "I pray that will be for many, many years."

His lips brushed against hers as he spoke, and the closing words of the minister echoed in Aimee's heart as she returned Jacob's kiss.

"And I declare that they shall be husband and wife together, till death parts them."

* * * * *

Dear Reader:

Thanks for reading my twentieth Love Inspired book. I always appreciate your letters of encouragement. It makes my day when someone writes that one of my books has brought them into a closer relationship with our Lord.

During my lifetime, I've baked a lot of pies, cookies, cakes and other pastries. In another book, I included a pie recipe in my letter, which seemed to be a hit with readers. Below is a recipe for some cookies mentioned in this book, which I've often made—the cookies are not only tasty, but pretty as well.

PEANUT BLOSSOMS

1 cup granulated sugar
1 cup packed brown sugar
1 cup margarine
1 cup creamy peanut butter
2 eggs
1/4 cup milk
2 tsp. vanilla
31/2 cups sifted flour
2 tsp. baking soda
1 tsp. salt
20 oz. Hershey's kisses

Cream sugars, butter, shortening and peanut butter. Beat in eggs, milk and vanilla. Sift flour, soda and salt together; stir into egg mixture. Shape into balls; roll in granulated sugar. Place on greased cookie sheet. Bake at 350°F for 8 to 10 minutes. Remove from oven. Top each cookie with a chocolate kiss, pressing down until cookie cracks around edge. Bake 3 to 5 minutes more. Yields 6 dozen.

Enjoy!

Irene B. Brand

QUESTIONS FOR DISCUSSION

1. This book has much to say about forgiveness. Jacob found it difficult to forgive his father who had abandoned him. Do you believe that his attitude about this situation was a normal reaction? Do you know children who have been abandoned by their parents who have also carried their unforgiving attitude into adulthood? What scriptures do you think would be applicable to their situation?

2. Aimee found it difficult to forgive herself because she believed that she hadn't met her husband's needs. Have you or anyone whom you know reacted to post-pregnancy in much the same way? How did you handle it?

3. Another issue in this book is the heroine's daughter's rebellion. Do you agree with Aimee's methods of tough love to curb Samantha's spirit? What would you have done in Aimee's situation?

4. Aimee blamed herself for Samantha's defiance. Is it the parents' fault if a child rebels, after the parents have done their best to teach her right from wrong? Discuss Proverbs 22:6.

5. Aimee believed that her failure as a mother could be attributed to her neglect of her Christian faith—for example, she had taught Samantha that school and social activities are more important than going to church. Is this a trend in modern society? How can parents change this trend as they rear their children?

6. Aimee found a closer relationship to God when she attended the Spiritual Growth Conference. Share with others an experience when you've grown closer to God in such a setting. Discuss Psalm 46:10a.

7. Erica was Aimee's best friend. What characteristics of friendship did Erica exhibit that you have found, or would like to find, in a friend?

8. The title of the book indicates that Aimee and Jacob were made for each other. What does "made for each other" suggest to you? Have you ever known a couple about whom you could say, "They were meant for each other"? If so, why did you think that?

9. Of all the issues that kept Aimee and Jacob separated, which do you believe was the

hardest for them to overcome? Which was the easiest?

10. Were you surprised to find out the identity of the father of Megan's child? Why?

11. What character was your favorite and why?

12. What is the main message in Jesus's words in Matthew 6:14-15? Close your session by praying together the prayer that Jesus taught His disciples, Matthew 6:9-13.

13. Considering the personalities of Jacob, Aimee and Samantha, what difficulties might have to be overcome before they can truly become a family?

Love Inspired®

SUSPENSE
RIVETING INSPIRATIONAL ROMANCE

Watch for our new series of
edge-of-your-seat suspense novels.
These contemporary tales
of intrigue and romance
feature Christian characters
facing challenges to their faith...
and their lives!

**Steeple
Hill**®

Visit:
www.SteepleHill.com

LISUSDIR07R